Reggie

KID PENGUIN

ABOUT THIS BOOK

This book was edited by Esther Cajahuaringa, art directed by David Caplan, and designed by Prashansa Thapa. The production was supervised by Bernadette Flinn, and the production editor was Marisa Finkelstein. The text was set in the creator's hand-lettered font, and the display type was hand-lettered by the creator.

This book is a work of fiction. Names, characters, places, and incidents are the product of the author's imagination or are used fictitiously. Any resemblance to actual events, locales, or persons, living or dead, is coincidental. • Copyright © 2023 by Jennifer de Oliveira • Cover illustration copyright © 2023 by Jennifer de Oliveira • Cover design by Prashansa Thapa • Cover copyright © 2023 by Hachette Book Group, Inc. • Hachette Book Group supports the right to free expression and the value of copyright. The purpose of copyright is to encourage writers and artists to produce the creative works that enrich our culture. • The scanning, uploading, and distribution of this book without permission is a theft of the author's intellectual property. If you would like permission to use material from the book (other than for review purposes), please contact permissions@hbgusa.com. Thank you for your support of the author's rights. • Little, Brown Ink • Hachette Book Group • 1290 Avenue of the Americas, New York, NY 10104 • Visit us at LBYR.com • First Edition: June 2023 • Little, Brown Ink is an imprint of Little, Brown and Company. The Little, Brown Ink name and logo are trademarks of Hachette Book Group, Inc. • The publisher is not responsible for websites (or their content) that are not owned by the publisher. • Little, Brown and Company books may be purchased in bulk for business, educational, or promotional use. For information, please contact your local bookseller or the Hachette Book Group Special Markets Department at special.markets@hbgusa.com. • Library of Congress Cataloging-in-Publication Data • Names: Oliveira, Jen de, author, illustrator. • Title: Reggie: kid penguin / Jen de Oliveira. • Description: First edition. | New York : Little, Brown and Company, 2023. | Series: Reggie ; 1 | Audience: Ages 4–8. | Summary: "Reginald 'Reggie' Guinn is a kid penguin who is equal parts playful, curious, and cantankerous, and gets into everyday adventures at school, home, and his neighborhood." —Provided by publisher. • Identifiers: LCCN 2021051008 | ISBN 9780759557550 (hardcover) | ISBN 9780759557567 (trade paperback) | ISBN 9780759557543 (ebook) • Subjects: CYAC: Graphic novels. | Penguins—Fiction. | LCGFT: Graphic novels. • Classification: LCC PZ7.7.O427 Re 2023 | DDC 741.5/973—dc23/eng/20220201 • LC record available at https://lccn.loc.gov/2021051008 • ISBNs: 978-0-7595-5755-0 (hardcover), 978-0-7595-5756-7 (pbk.), 978-0-7595-5754-3 (ebook), 978-0-316-38422-3 (ebook), 978-0-316-38427-8 (ebook) • PRINTED IN CHINA • APS • Hardcover: 10 9 8 7 6 5 4 3 2 1 • Paperback: 10 9 8 7 6 5 4 3 2 1

FOR MY MAMA, VICKEY

Reggie

KID PENGUIN

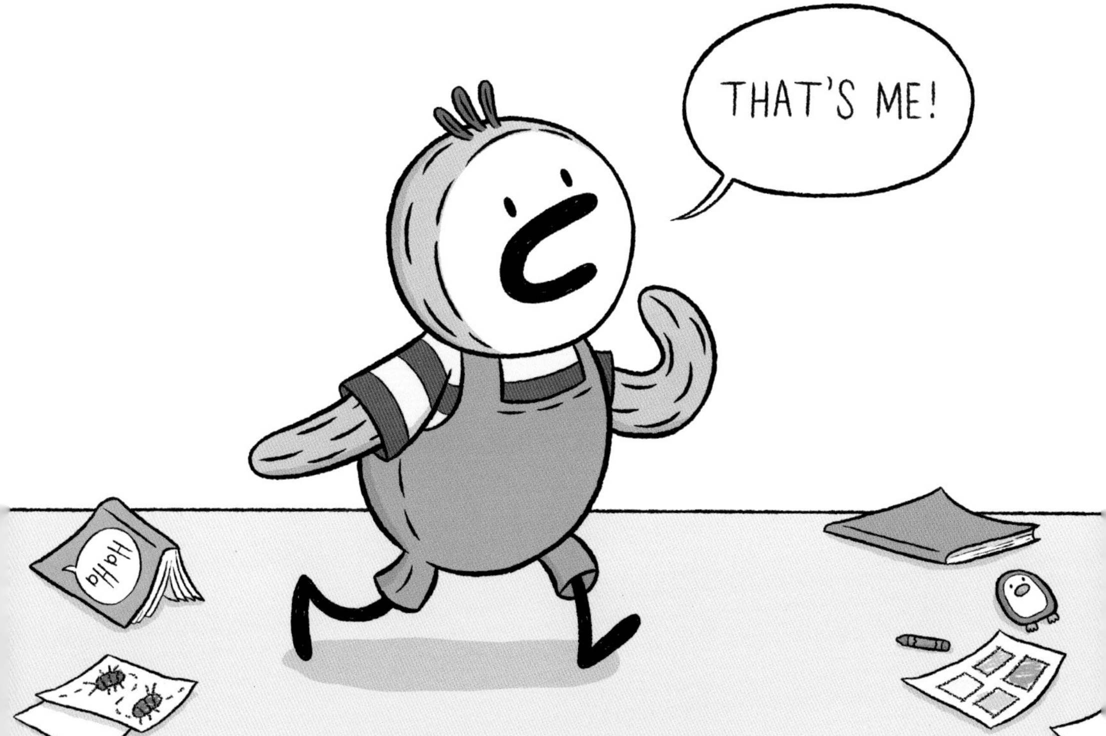
THAT'S ME!
HaHa

JEN de OLIVEIRA

LB INK

LITTLE, BROWN AND COMPANY
NEW YORK • BOSTON

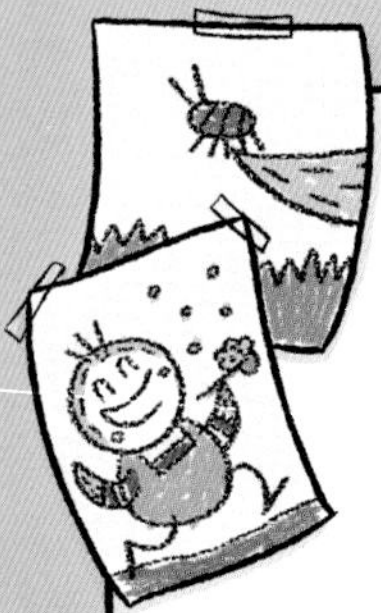

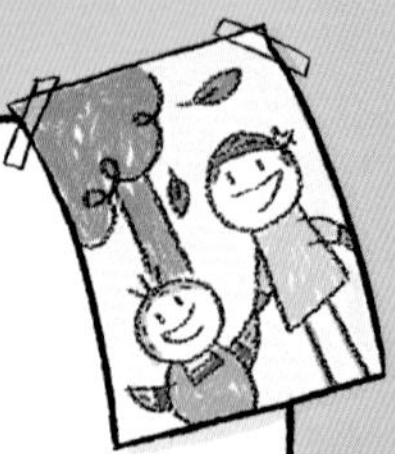

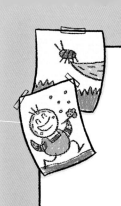

Stories

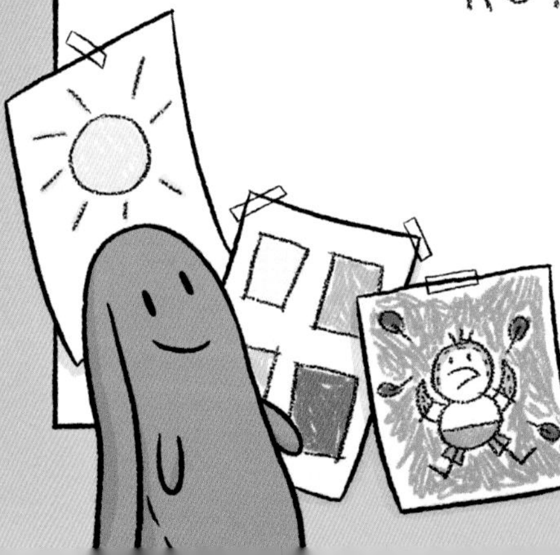

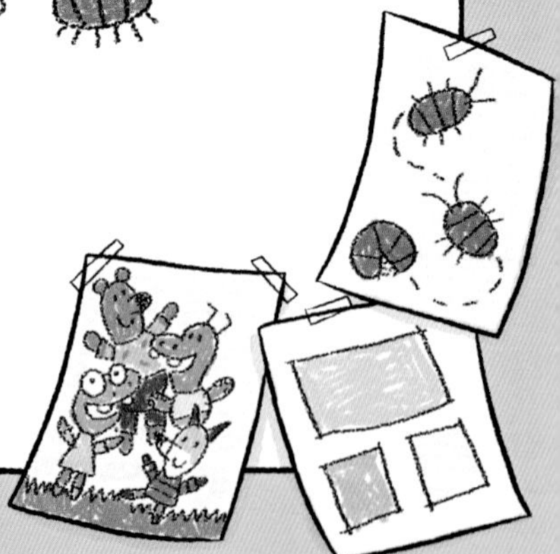

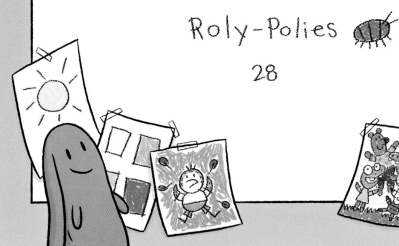

MY FAVORITE STORY IS...
ALL OF THEM!

The Portrait

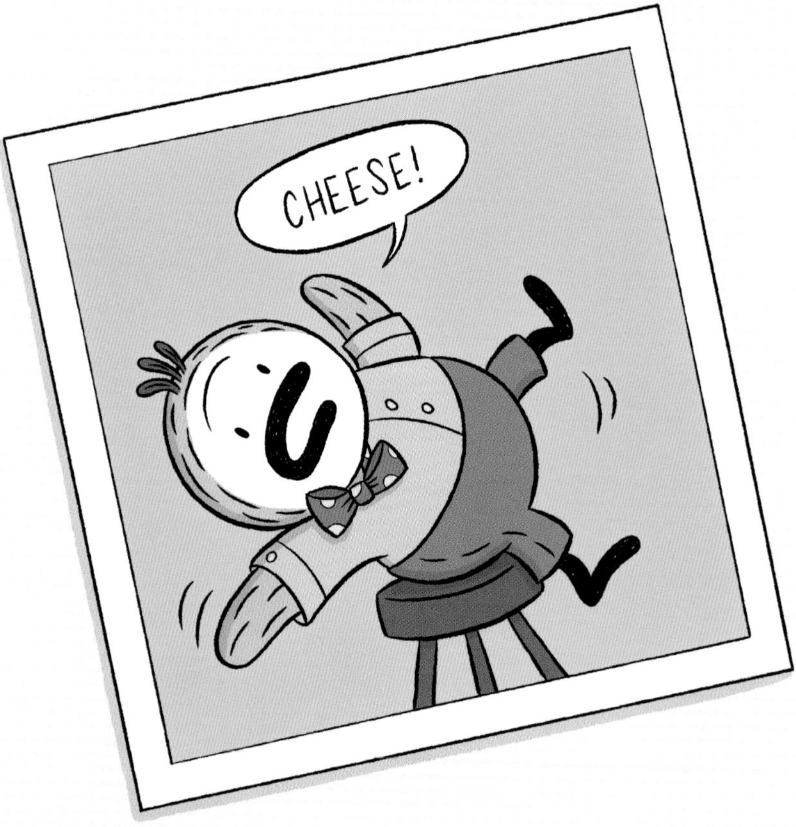
CHEESE!

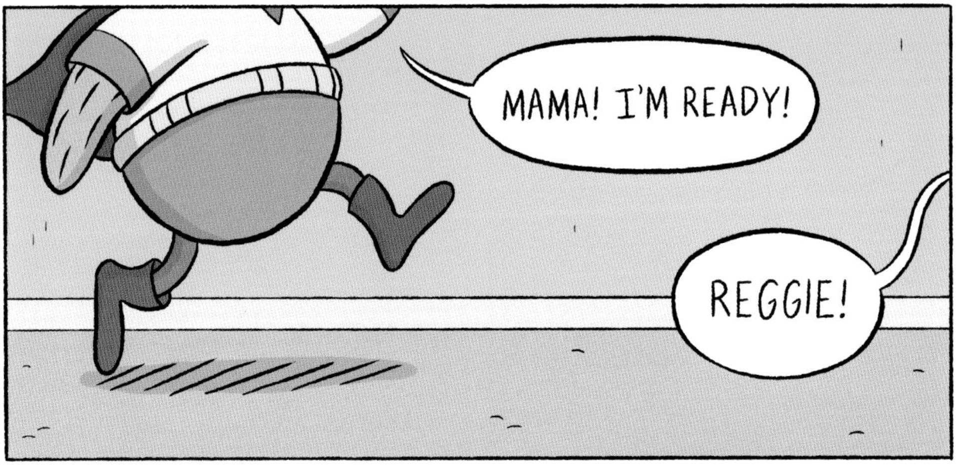
MAMA! I'M READY!
REGGIE!

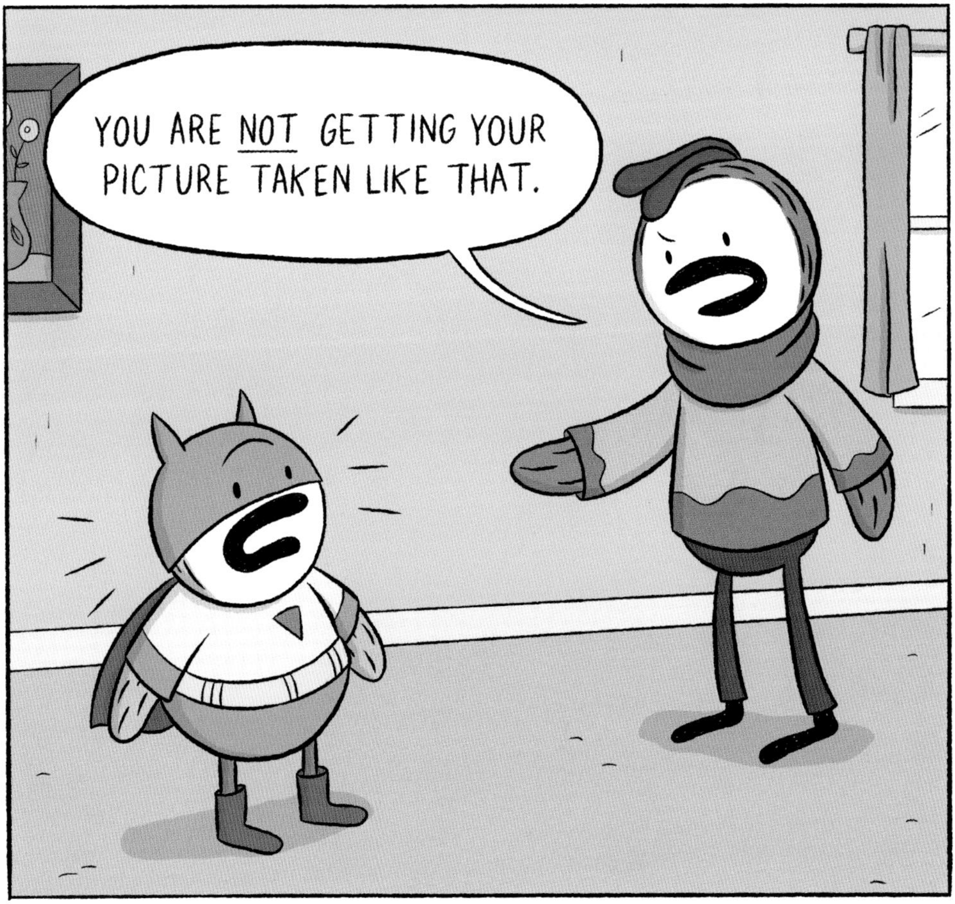
YOU ARE NOT GETTING YOUR PICTURE TAKEN LIKE THAT.

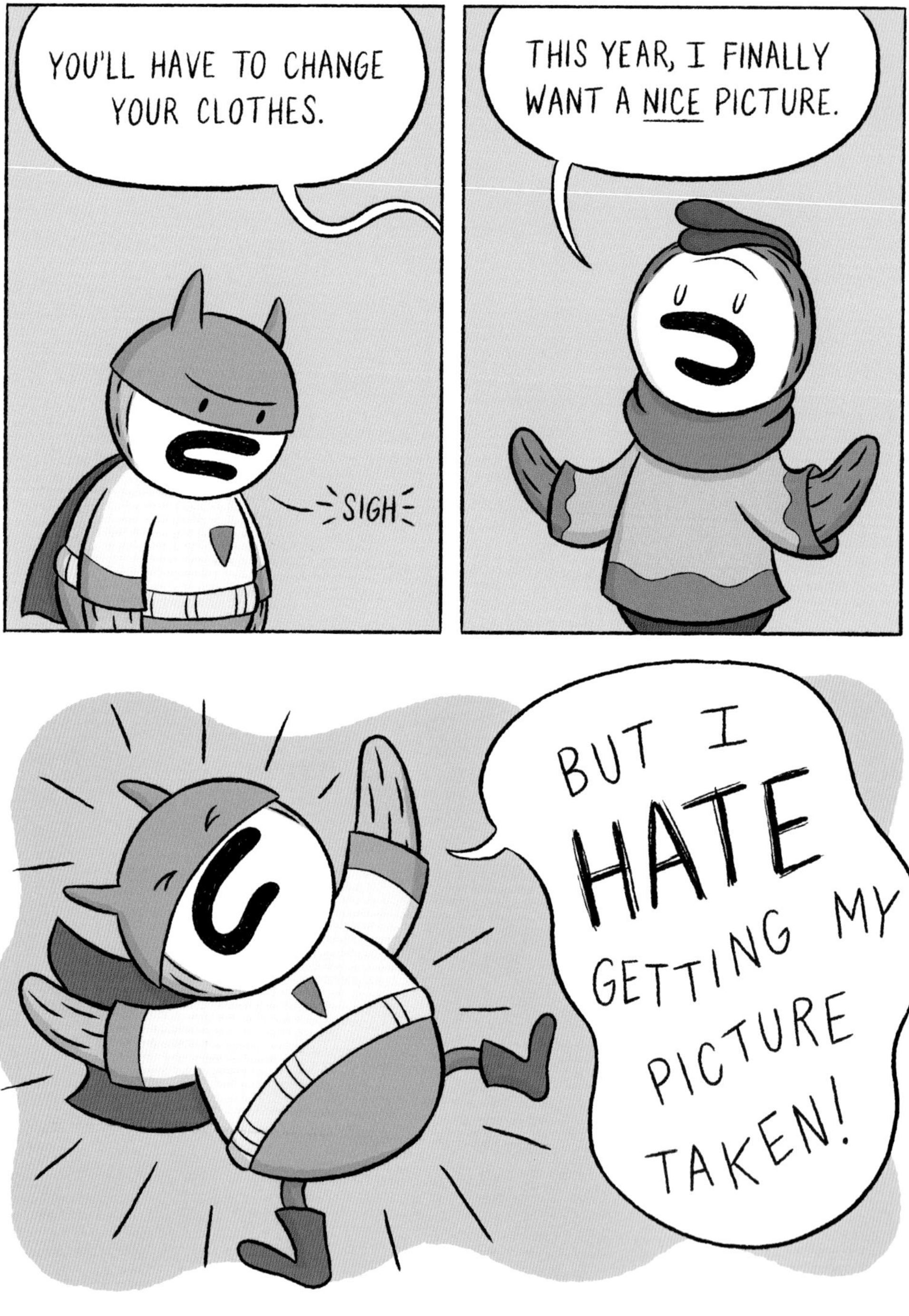
YOU'LL HAVE TO CHANGE YOUR CLOTHES.
SIGH
THIS YEAR, I FINALLY WANT A NICE PICTURE.
BUT I HATE GETTING MY PICTURE TAKEN!

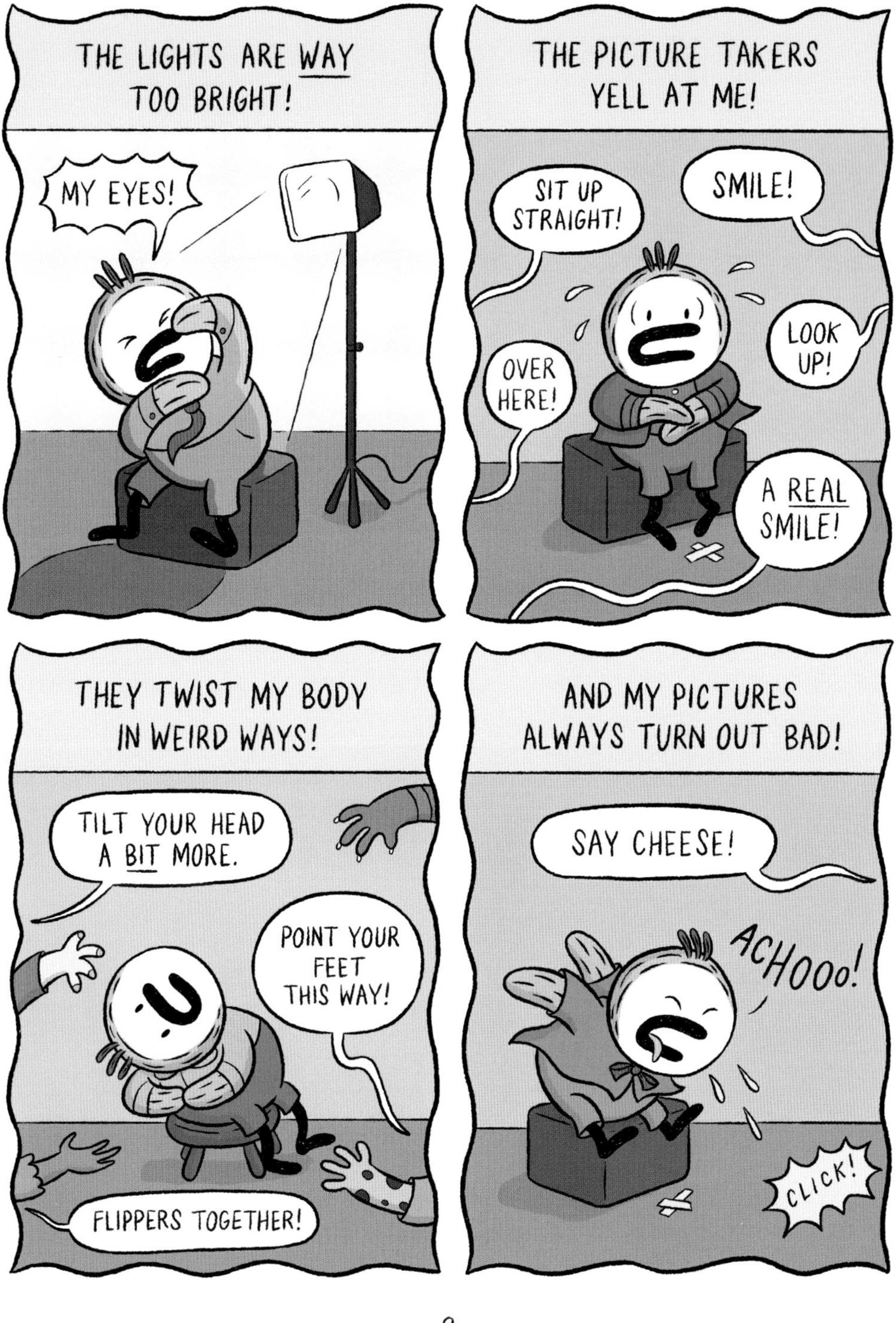
THE LIGHTS ARE WAY TOO BRIGHT!
MY EYES!
THE PICTURE TAKERS YELL AT ME!
SIT UP STRAIGHT!
SMILE!
OVER HERE!
LOOK UP!
A REAL SMILE!
THEY TWIST MY BODY IN WEIRD WAYS!
TILT YOUR HEAD A BIT MORE.
POINT YOUR FEET THIS WAY!
FLIPPERS TOGETHER!
AND MY PICTURES ALWAYS TURN OUT BAD!
SAY CHEESE!
ACHOOo!
CLICK!

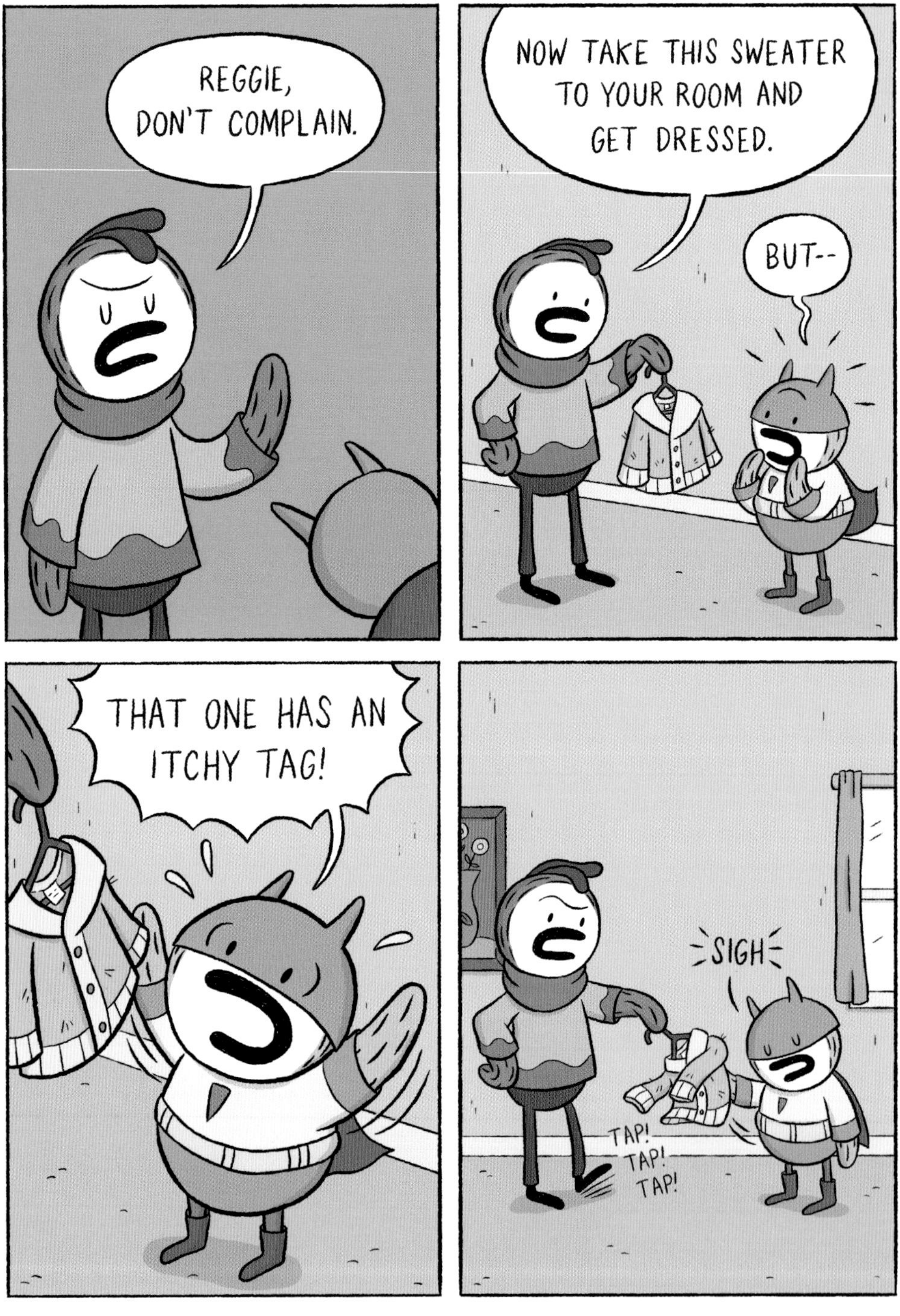
REGGIE, DON'T COMPLAIN.
NOW TAKE THIS SWEATER TO YOUR ROOM AND GET DRESSED.
BUT--
THAT ONE HAS AN ITCHY TAG!
SIGH
TAP! TAP! TAP!

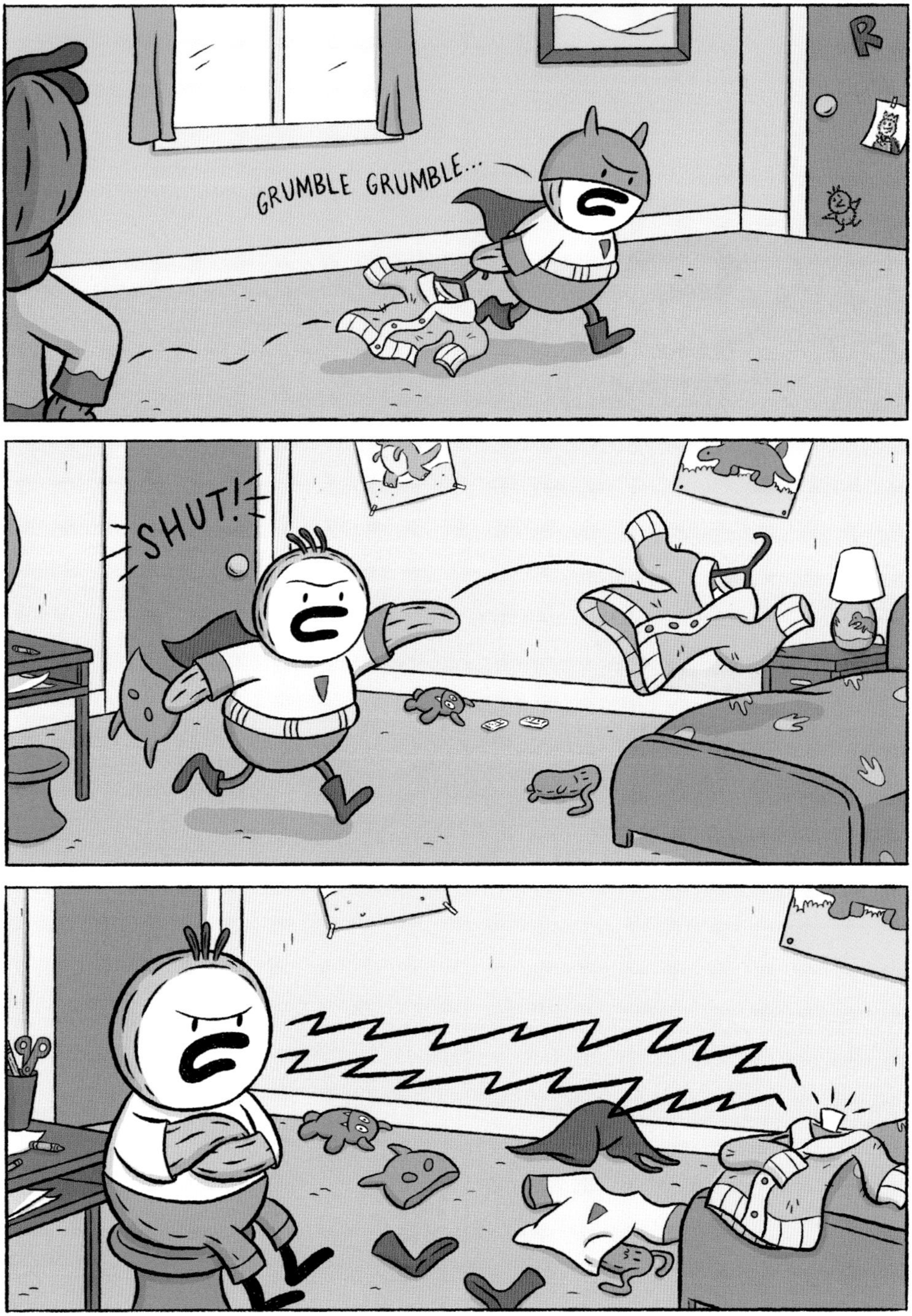
GRUMBLE GRUMBLE...
SHUT!

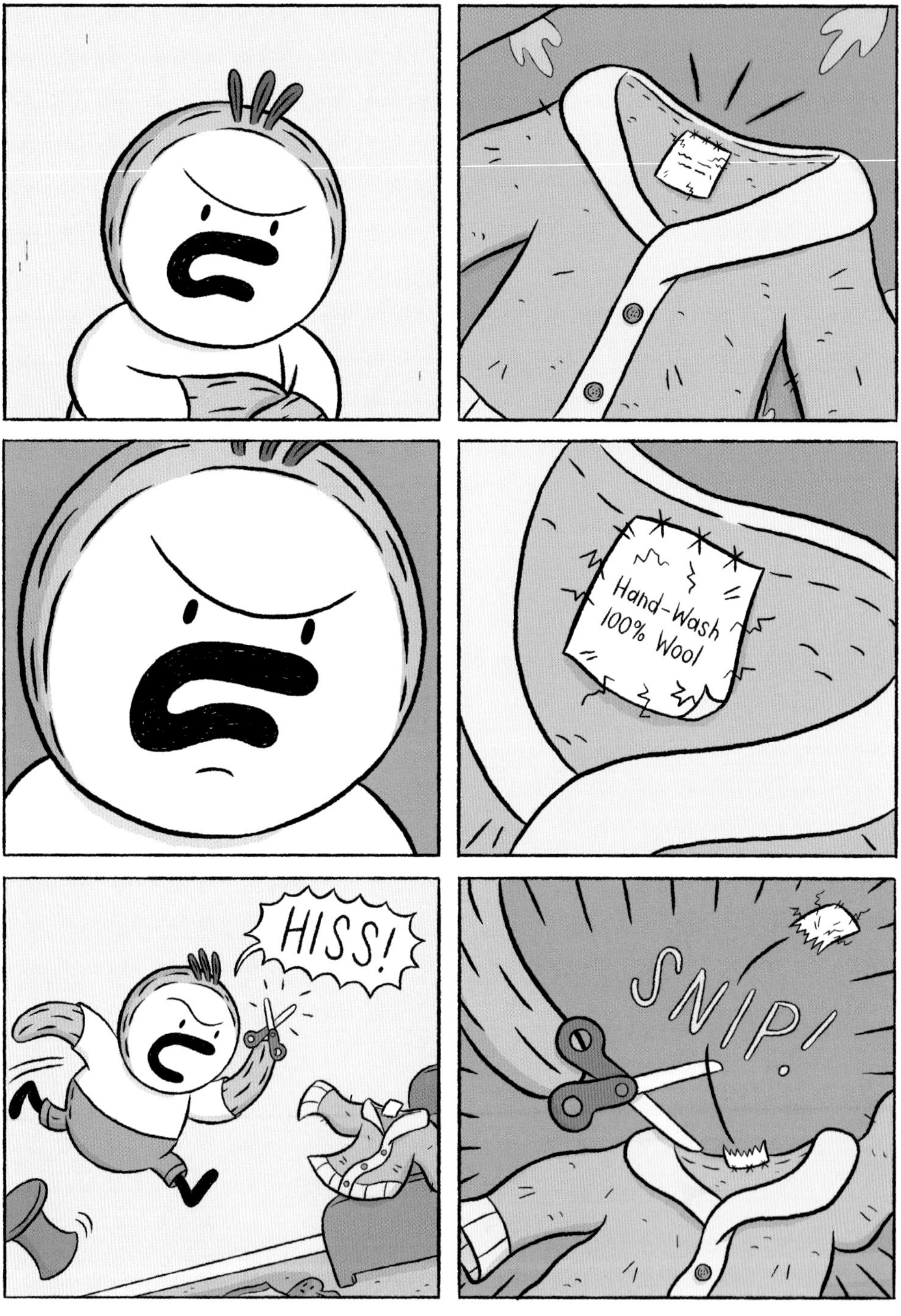
Hand-Wash
100% Wool
HISS!
SNIP!

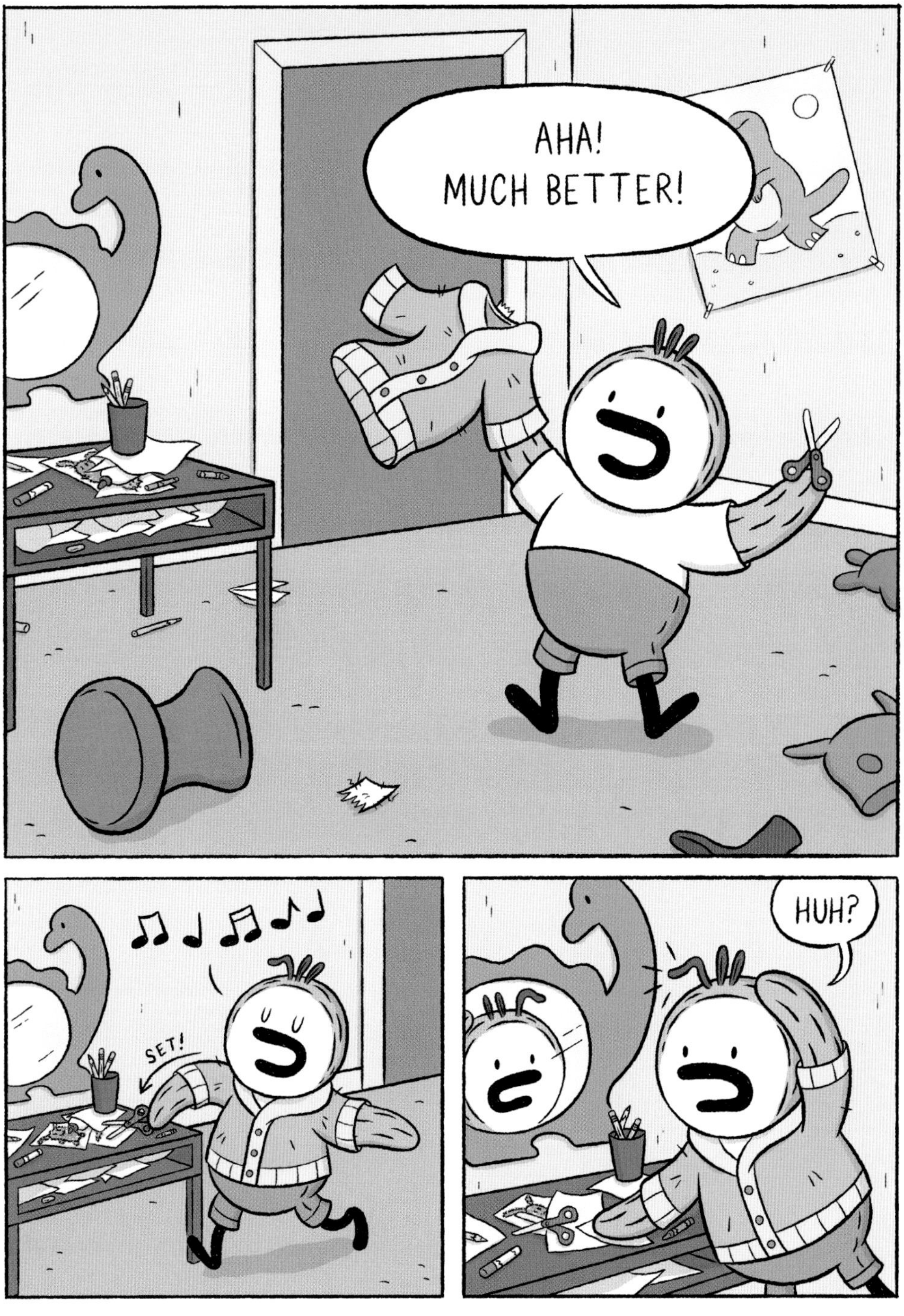
AHA!
MUCH BETTER!
SET!
HUH?

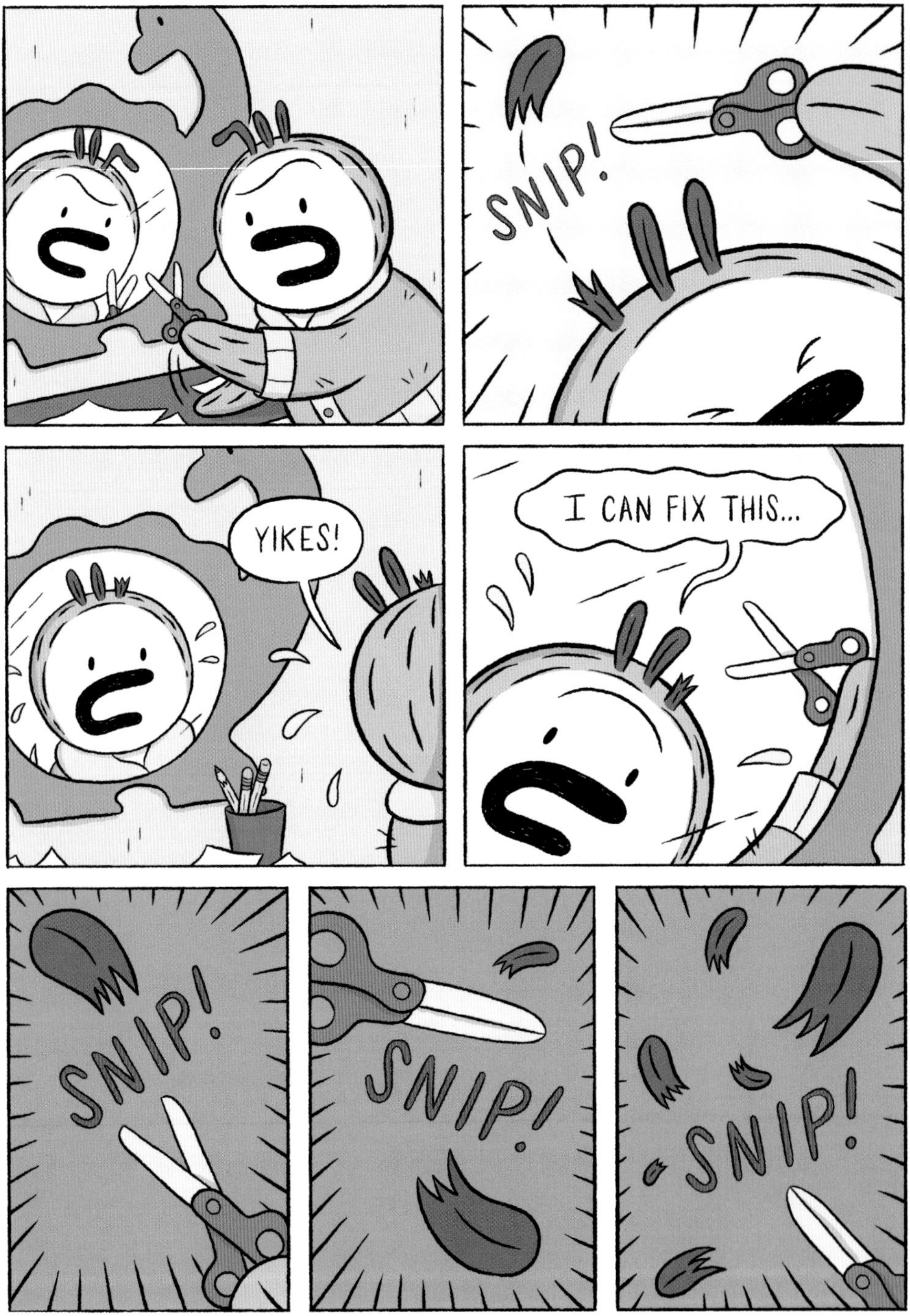
SNIP!
YIKES!
I CAN FIX THIS...
SNIP!
SNIP!
SNIP!

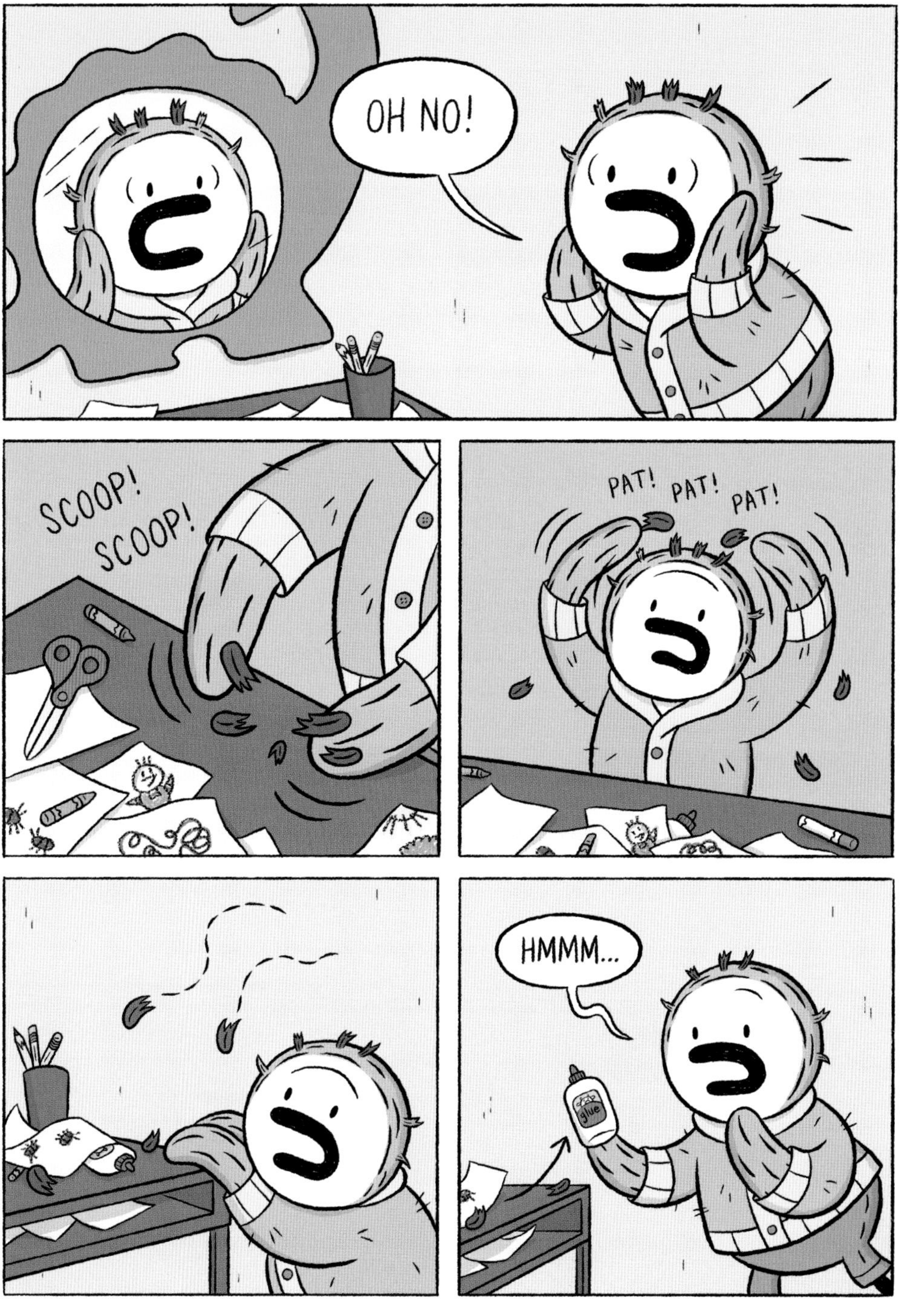
OH NO!
SCOOP!
SCOOP!
PAT!
PAT!
PAT!
HMMM...
glue

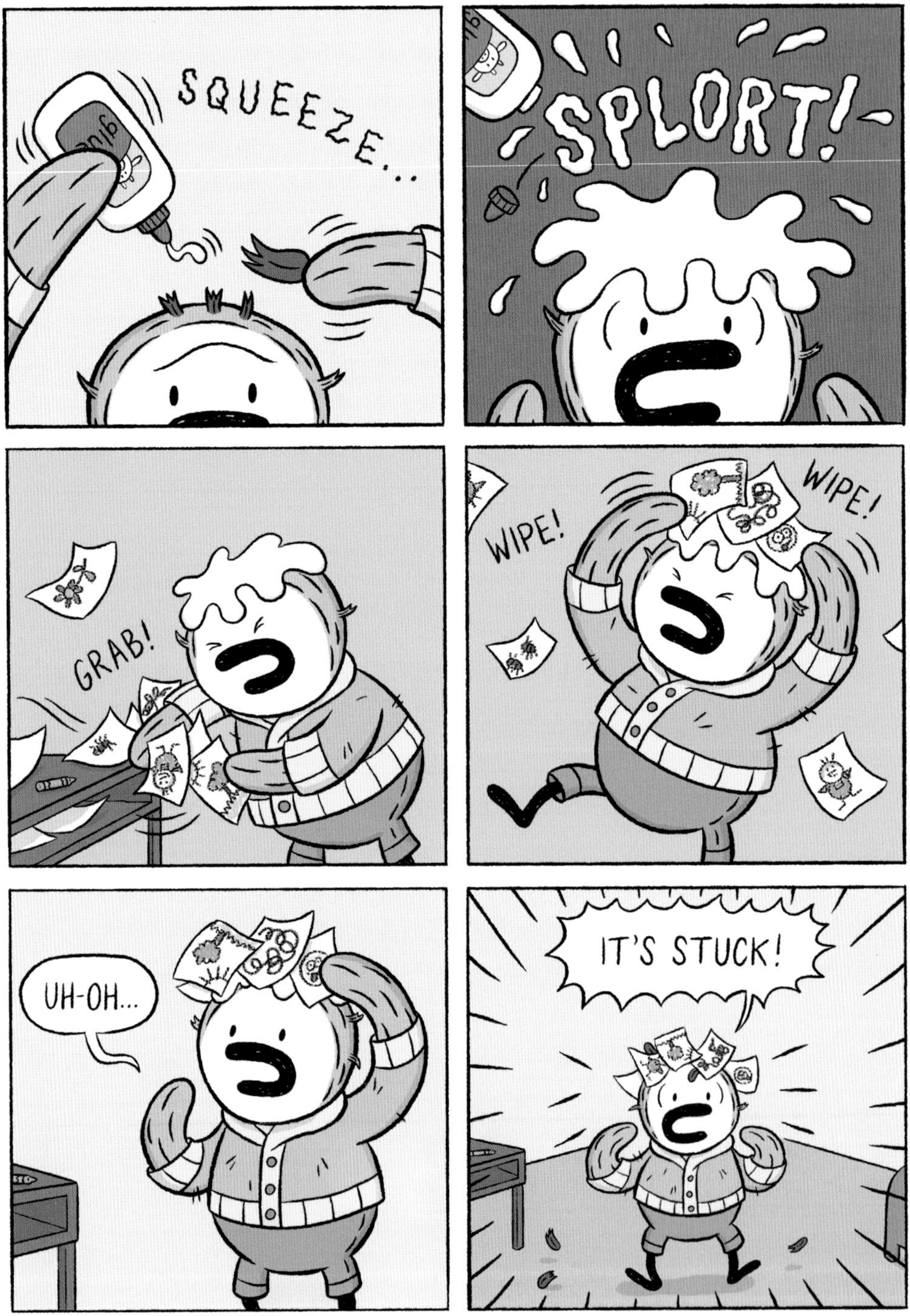
SQUEEZE...
glue
SPLORT!
GRAB!
WIPE!
WIPE!
UH-OH...
IT'S STUCK!

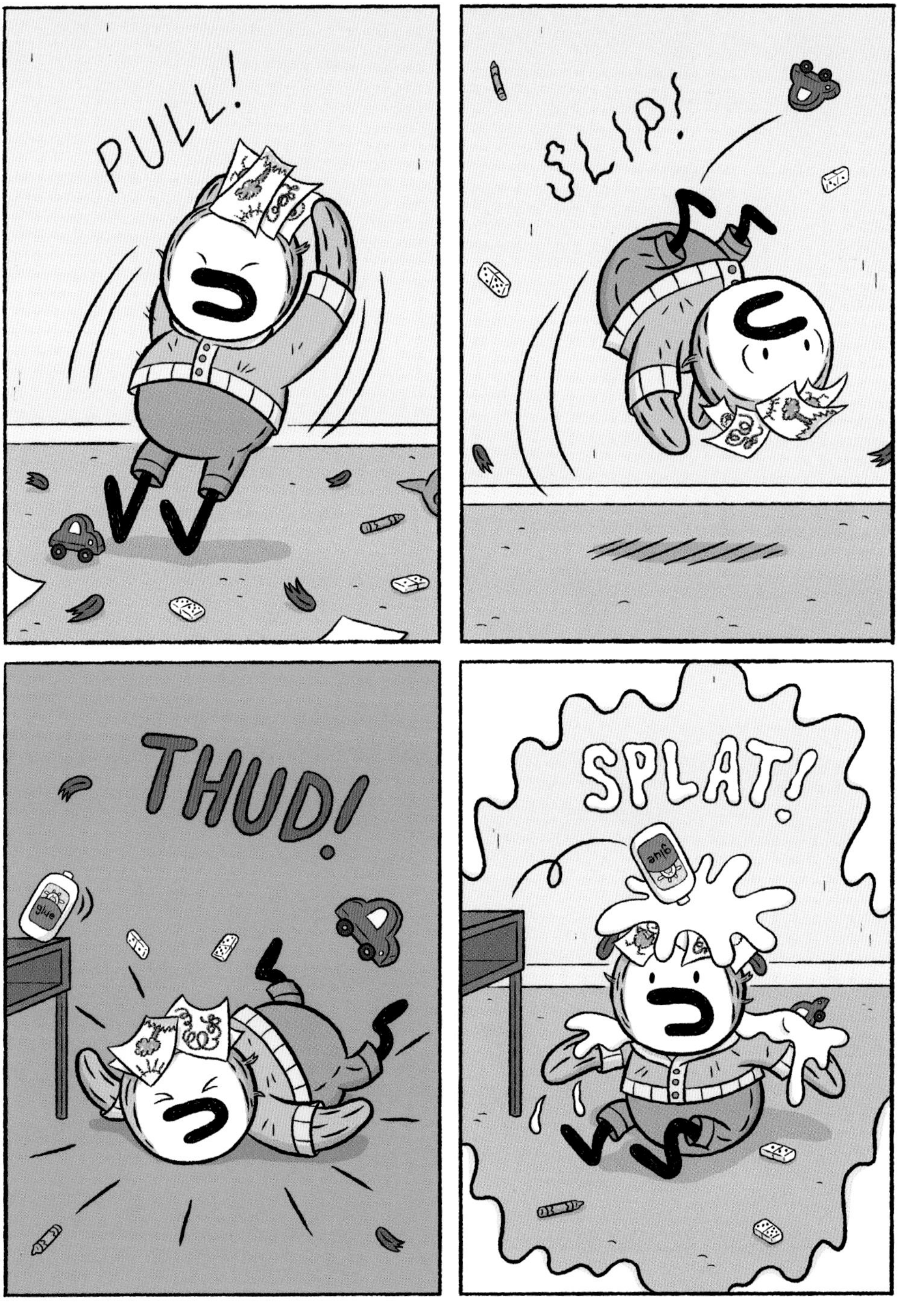
PULL!
SLIP!
THUD!
SPLAT!
glue

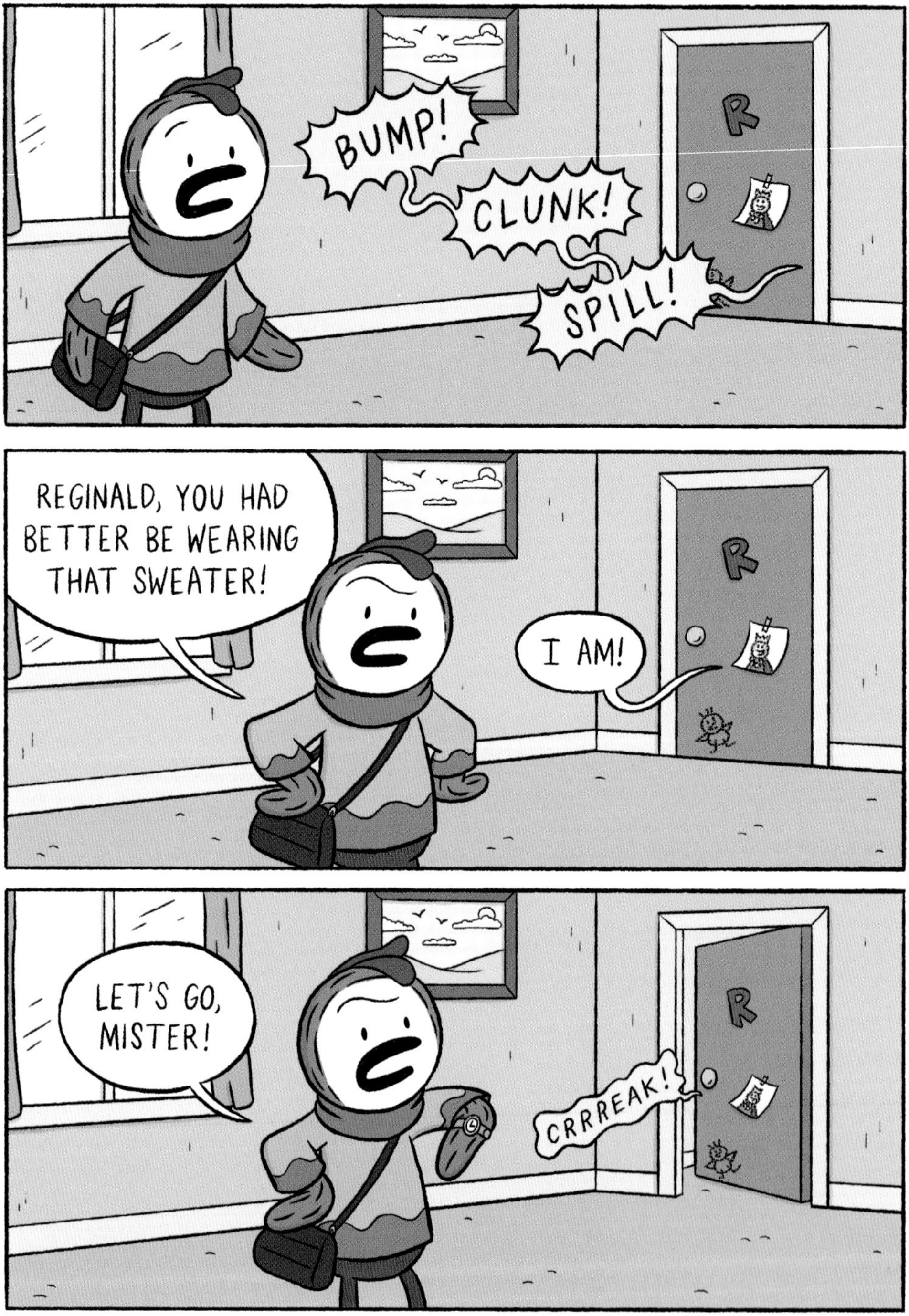
BUMP!
CLUNK!
SPILL!
REGINALD, YOU HAD BETTER BE WEARING THAT SWEATER!
I AM!
LET'S GO, MISTER!
CRRREAK!

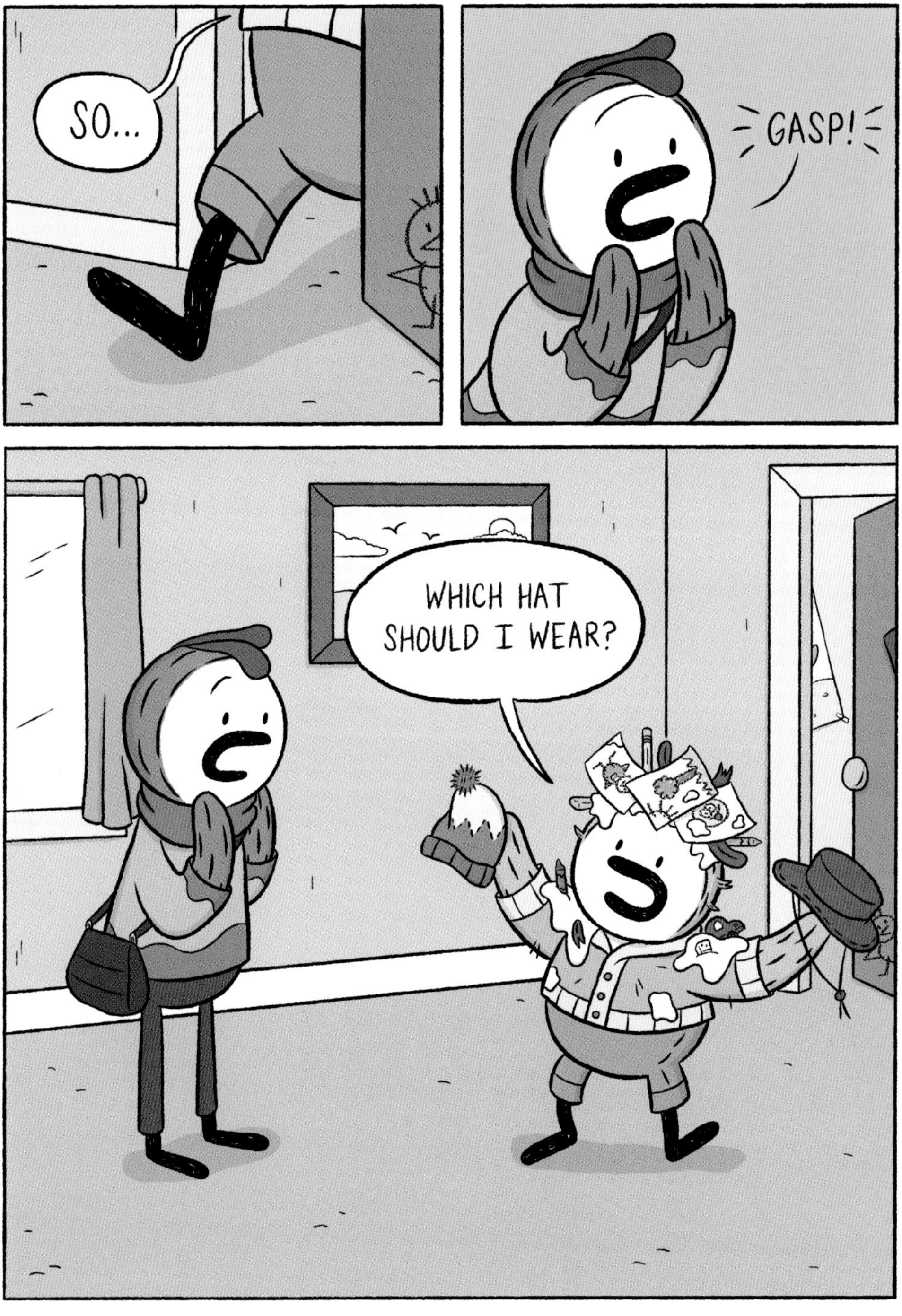
SO...
GASP!
WHICH HAT SHOULD I WEAR?

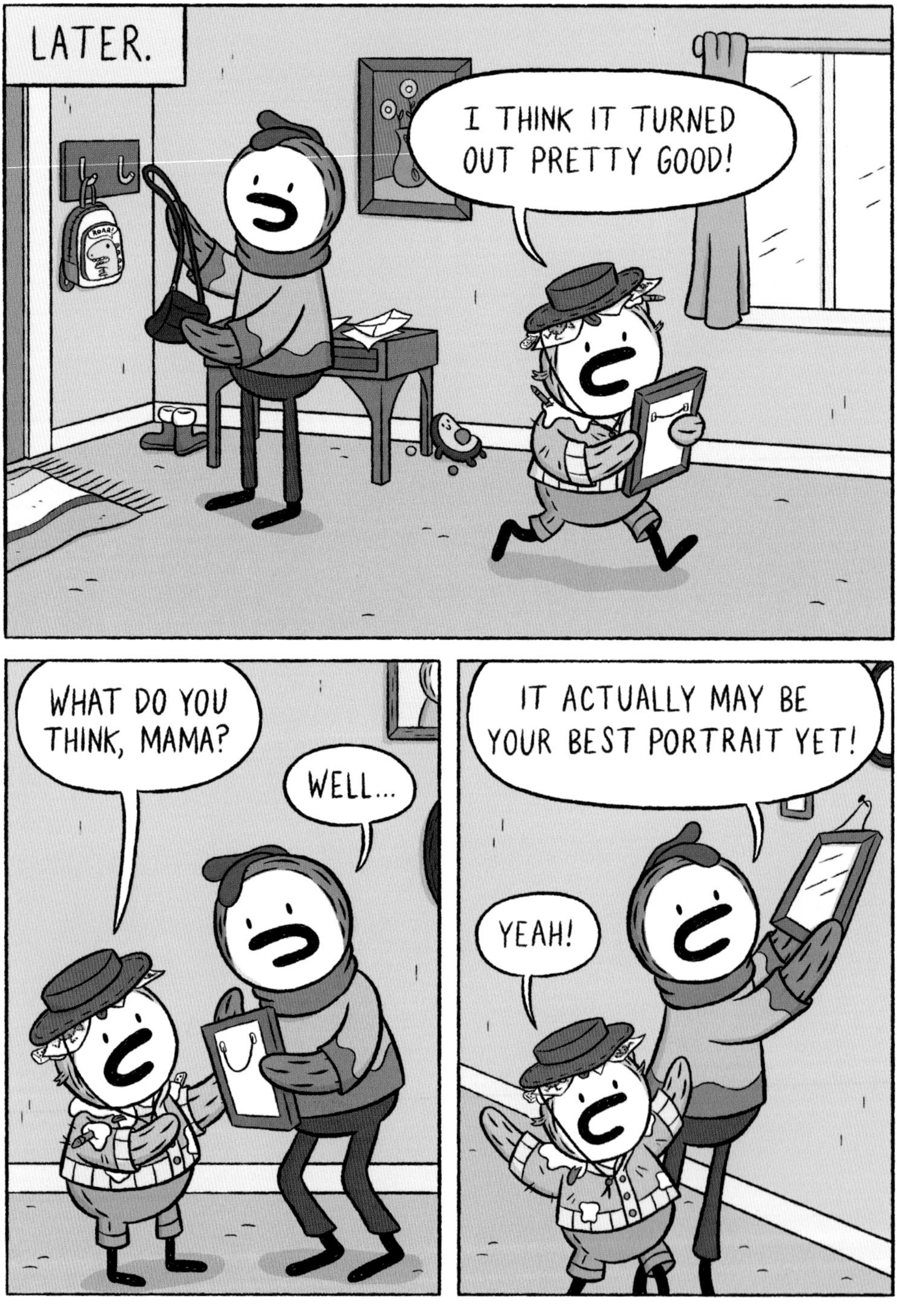
LATER.
I THINK IT TURNED OUT PRETTY GOOD!
WHAT DO YOU THINK, MAMA?
WELL...
IT ACTUALLY MAY BE YOUR BEST PORTRAIT YET!
YEAH!

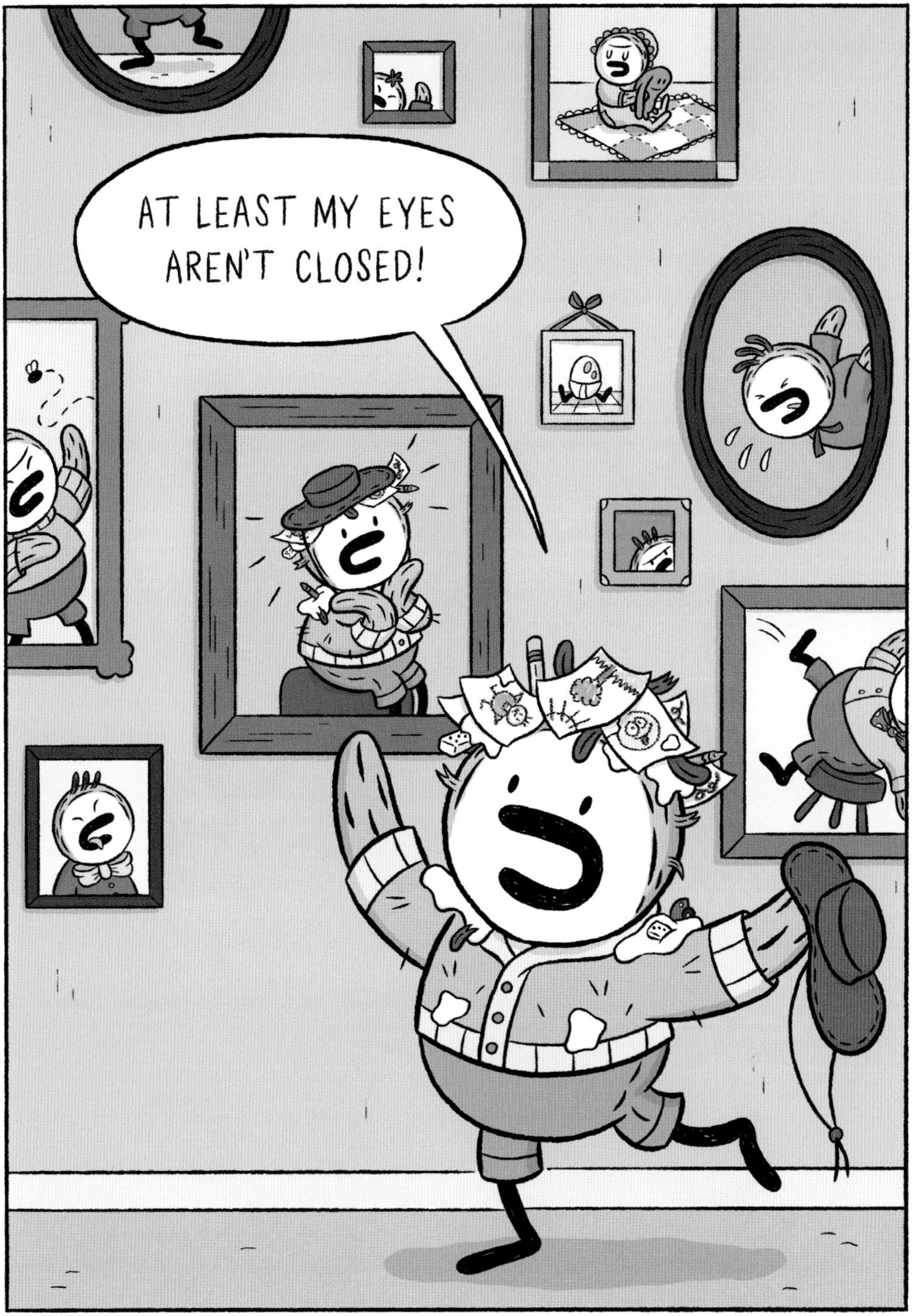
AT LEAST MY EYES AREN'T CLOSED!

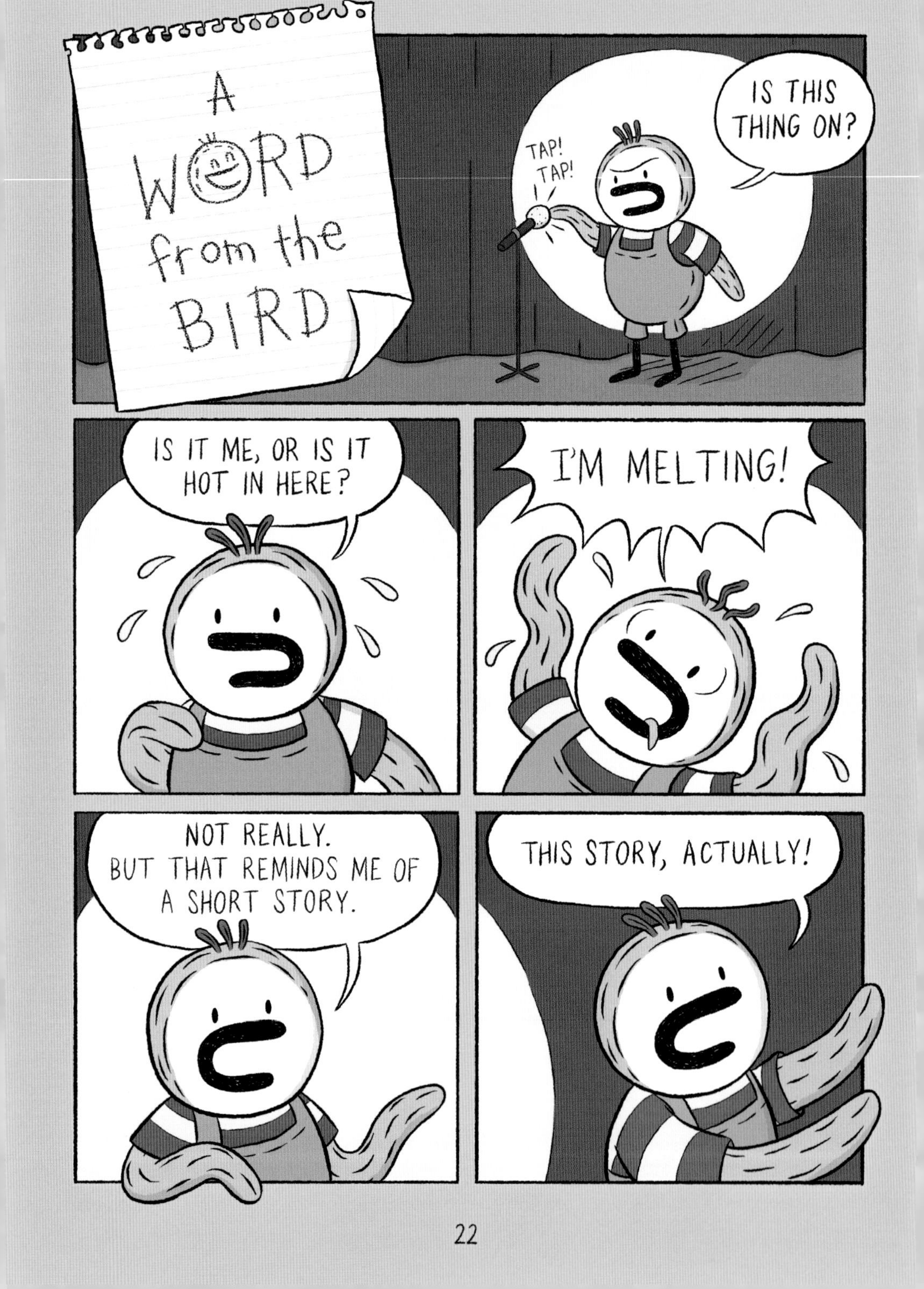
A WORD from the BIRD
TAP! TAP!
IS THIS THING ON?
IS IT ME, OR IS IT HOT IN HERE?
I'M MELTING!
NOT REALLY. BUT THAT REMINDS ME OF A SHORT STORY.
THIS STORY, ACTUALLY!

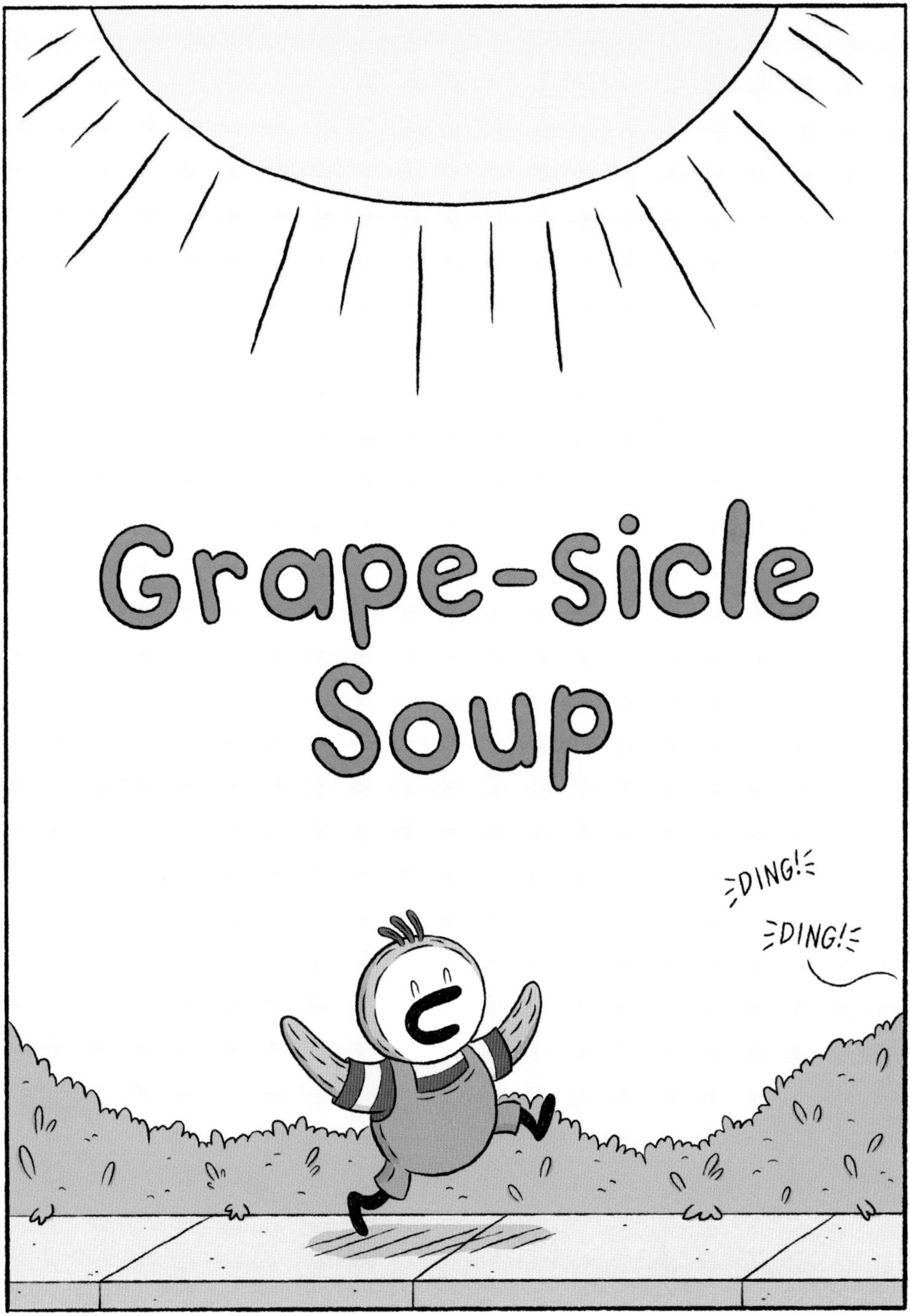
Grape-sicle Soup
DING!
DING!

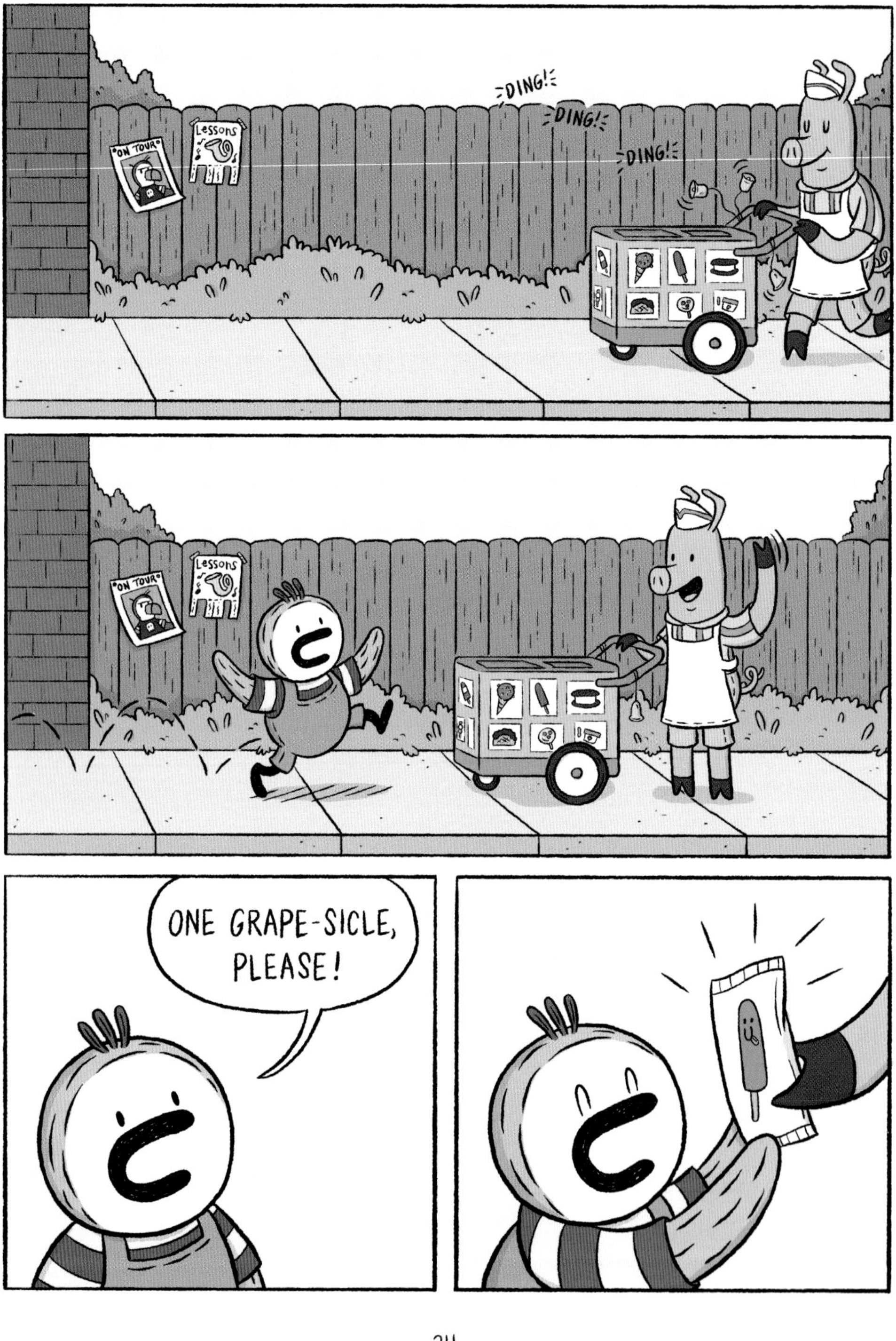
ON TOUR
Lessons
DING!
DING!
DING!
ON TOUR
Lessons
ONE GRAPE-SICLE, PLEASE!

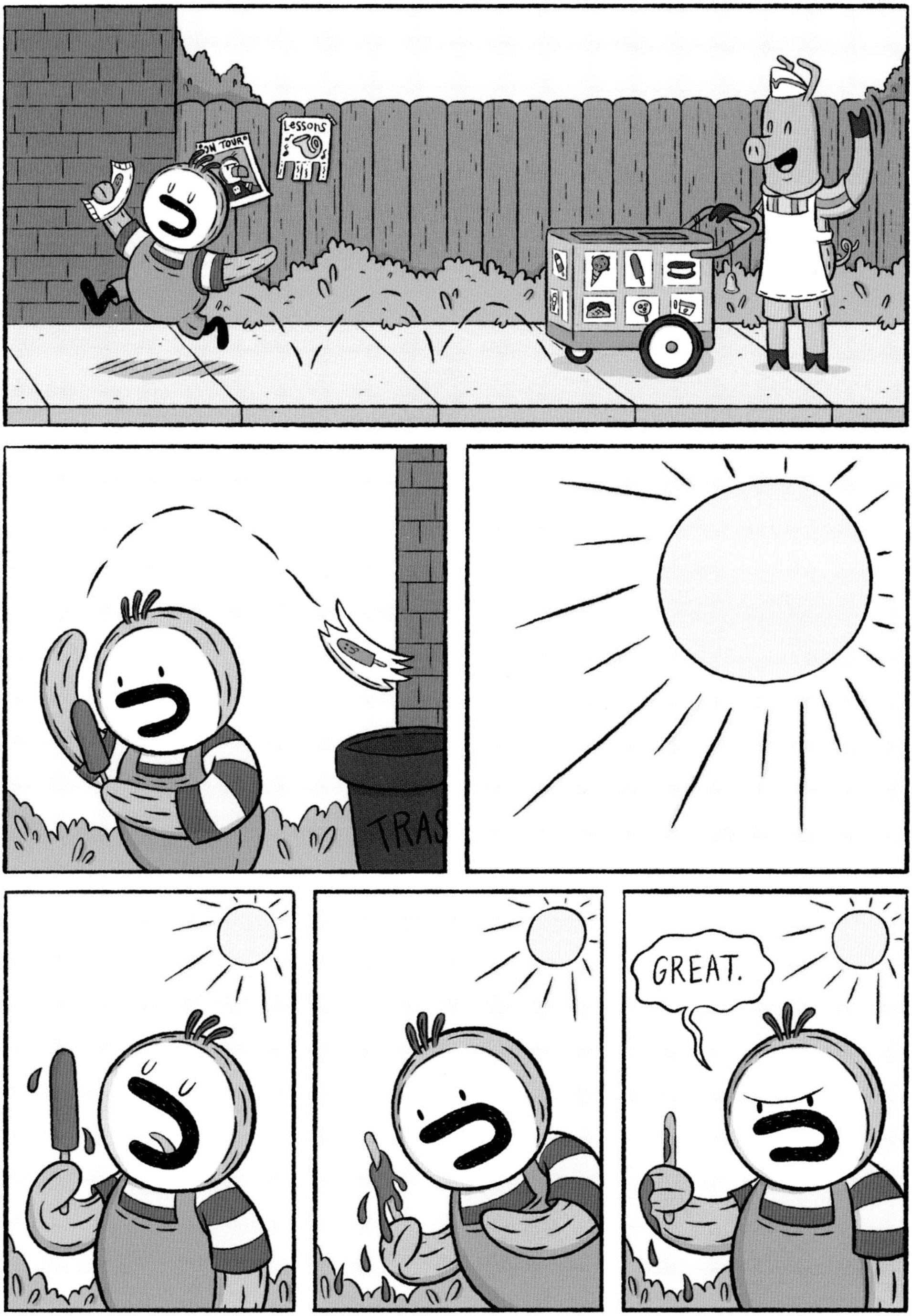

ON TOUR
Lessons
TRAS
GREAT.

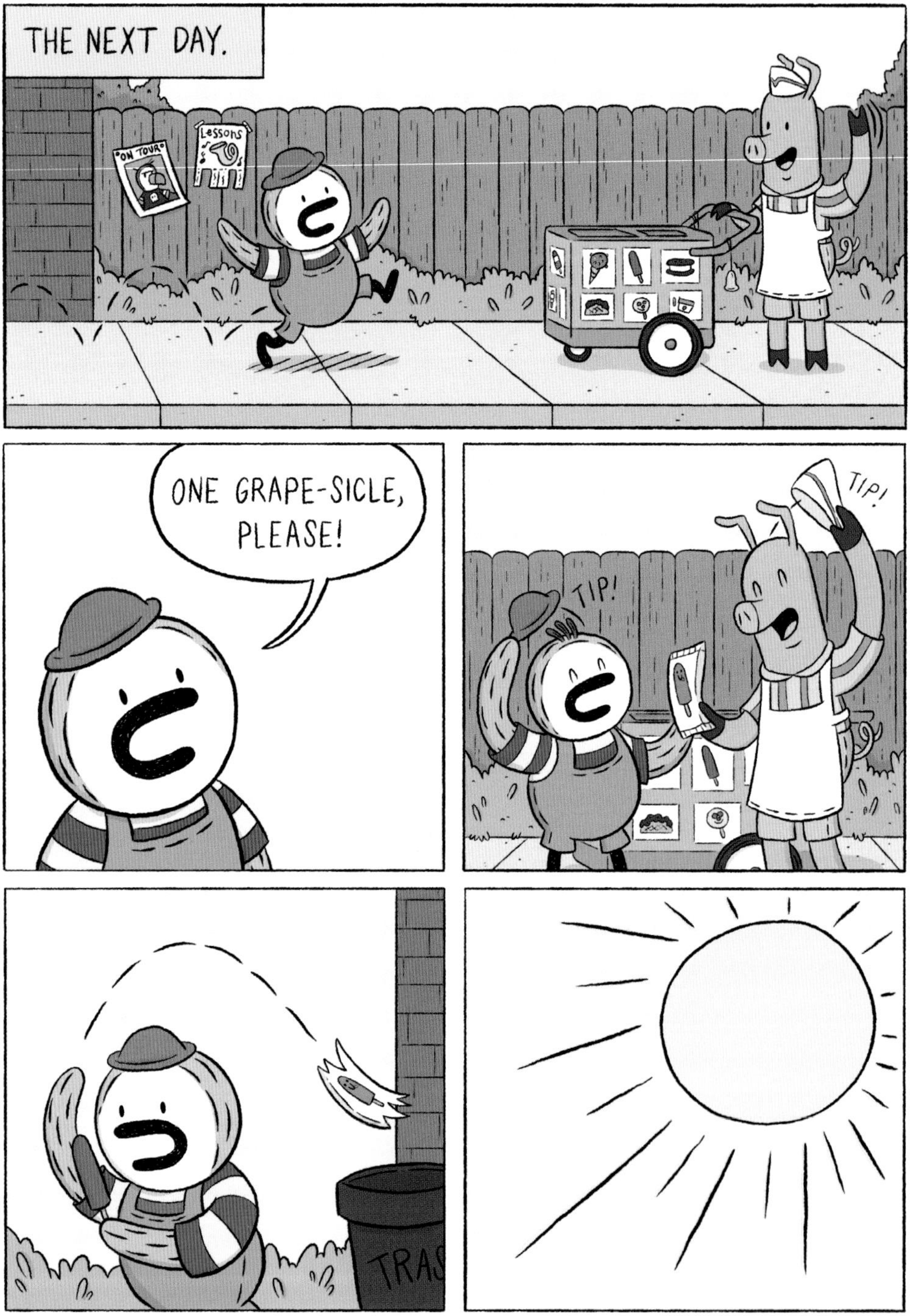
THE NEXT DAY.
ON TOUR
Lessons
ONE GRAPE-SICLE, PLEASE!
TIP!
TIP!
TRAS

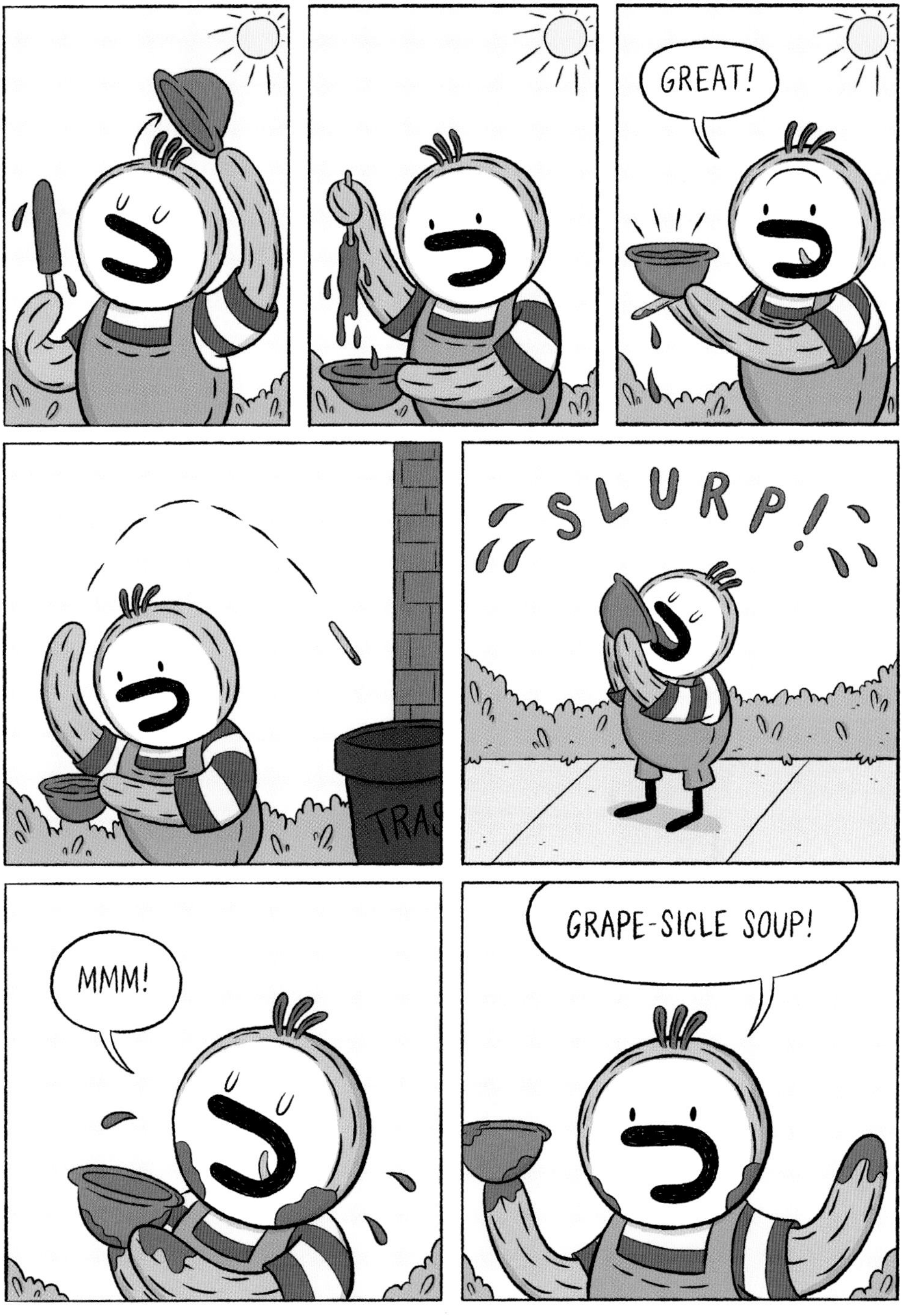
GREAT!
SLURP!
TRAS
MMM!
GRAPE-SICLE SOUP!

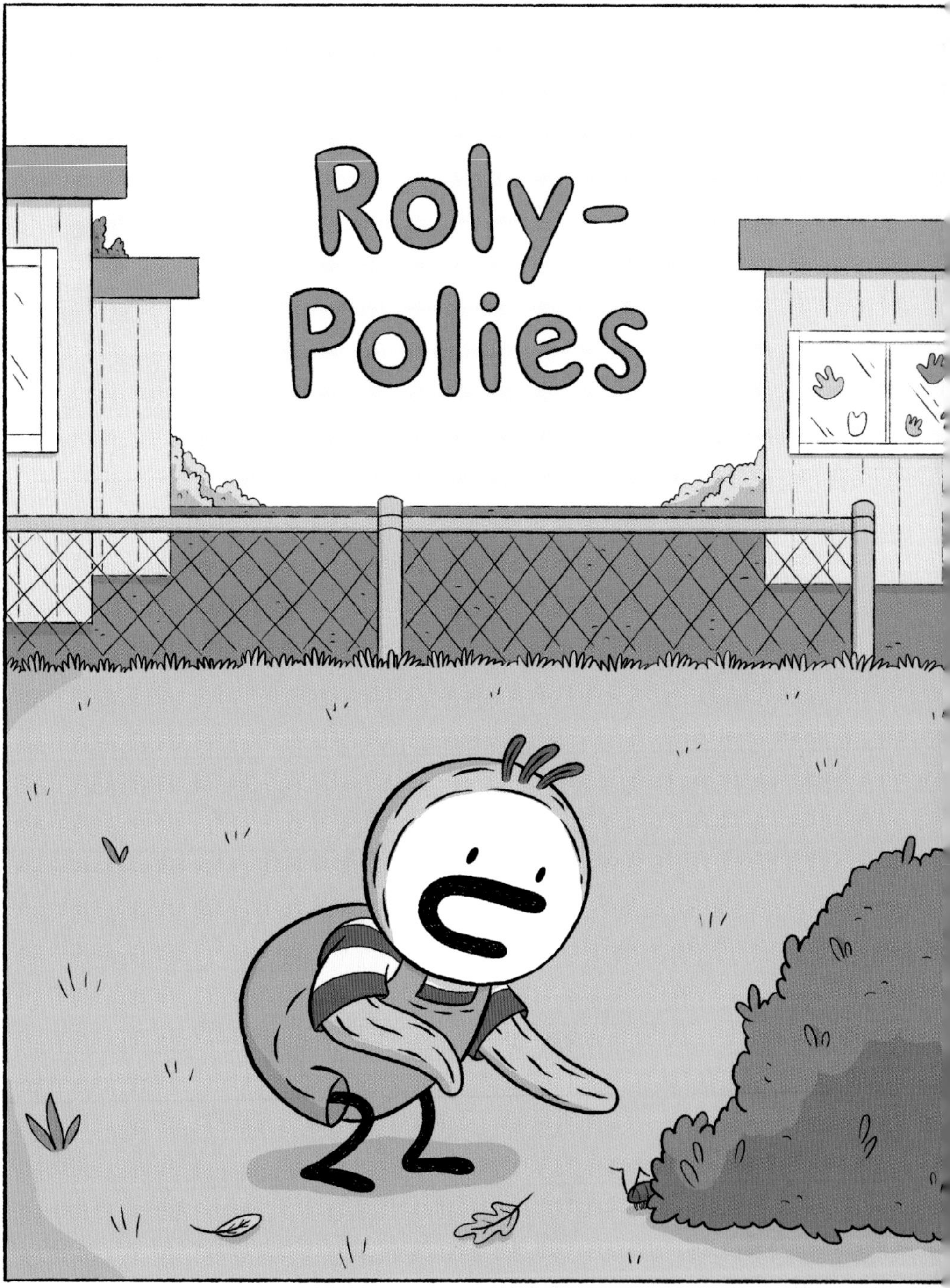
Roly-Polies

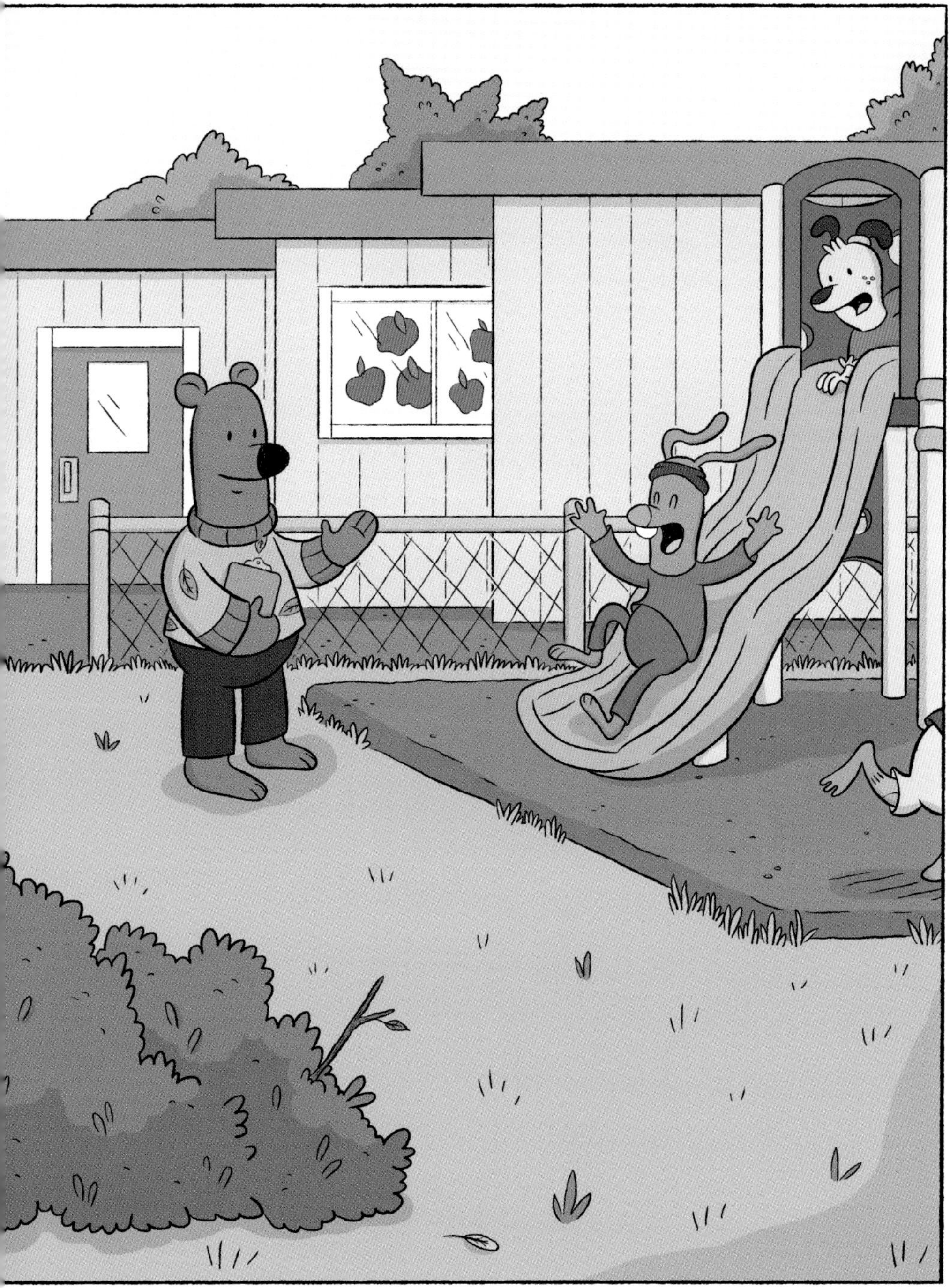

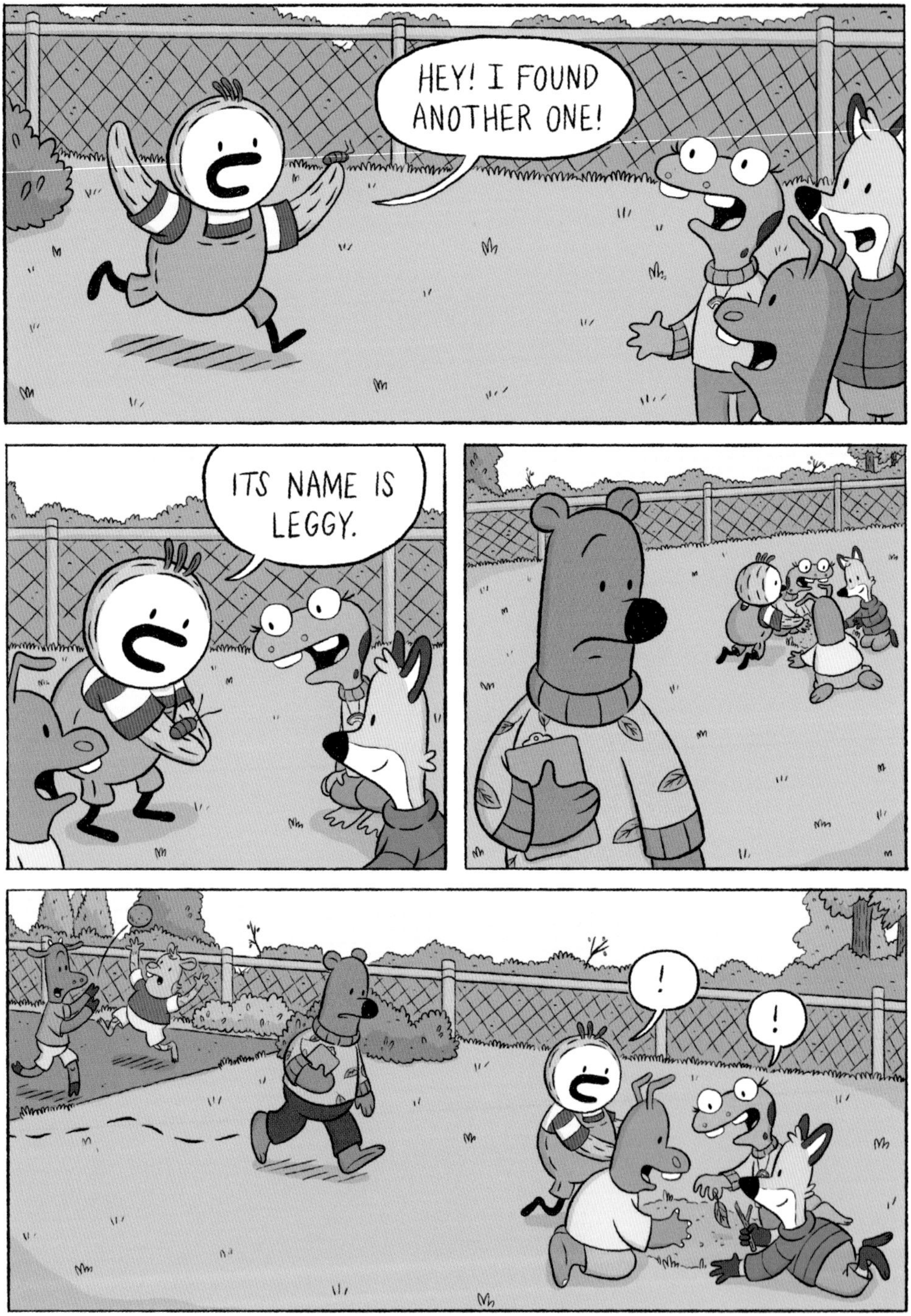
HEY! I FOUND ANOTHER ONE!
ITS NAME IS LEGGY.
!
!

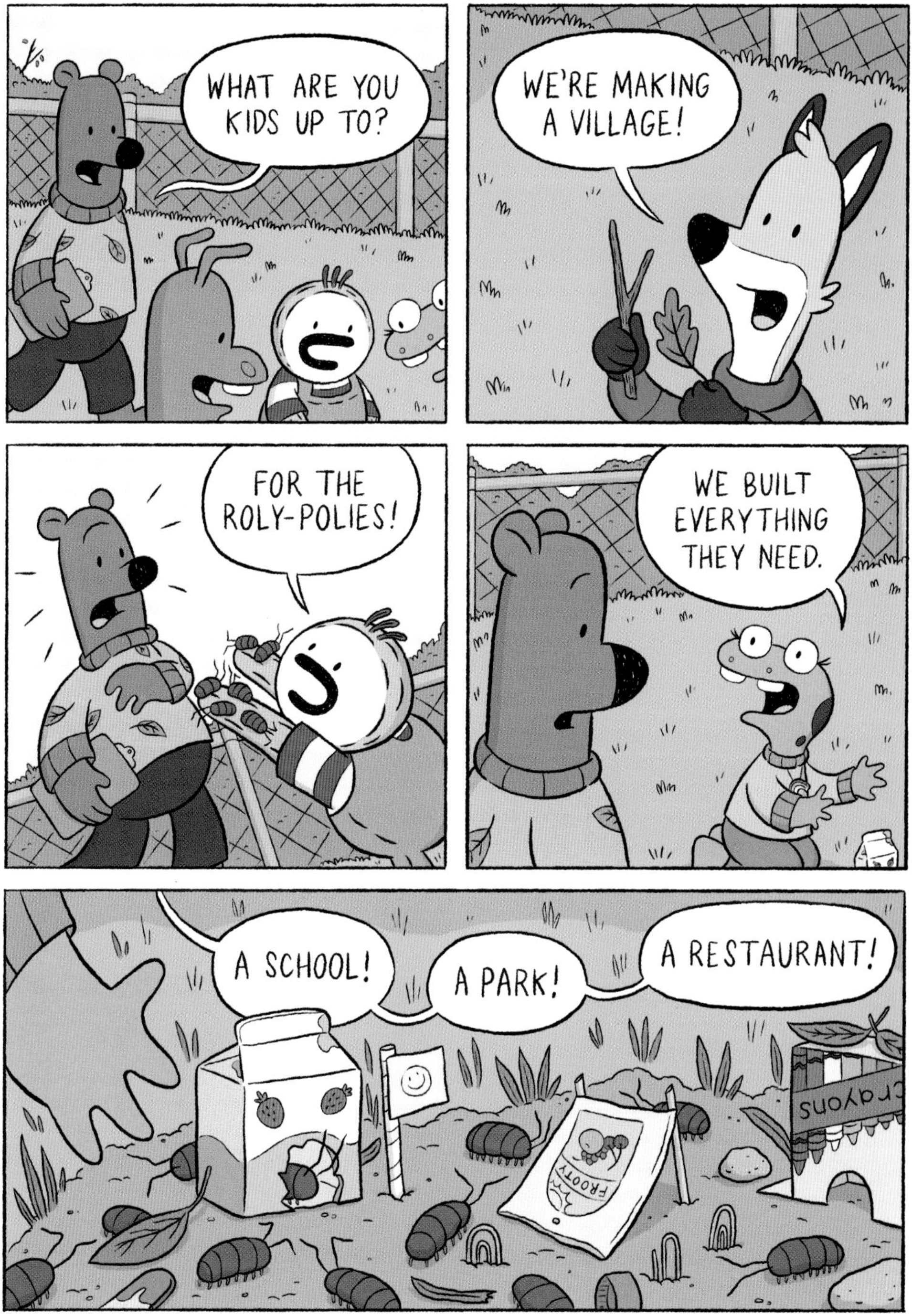
WHAT ARE YOU KIDS UP TO?
WE'RE MAKING A VILLAGE!
FOR THE ROLY-POLIES!
WE BUILT EVERYTHING THEY NEED.
A SCHOOL!
A PARK!
A RESTAURANT!
FROOTY
crayons

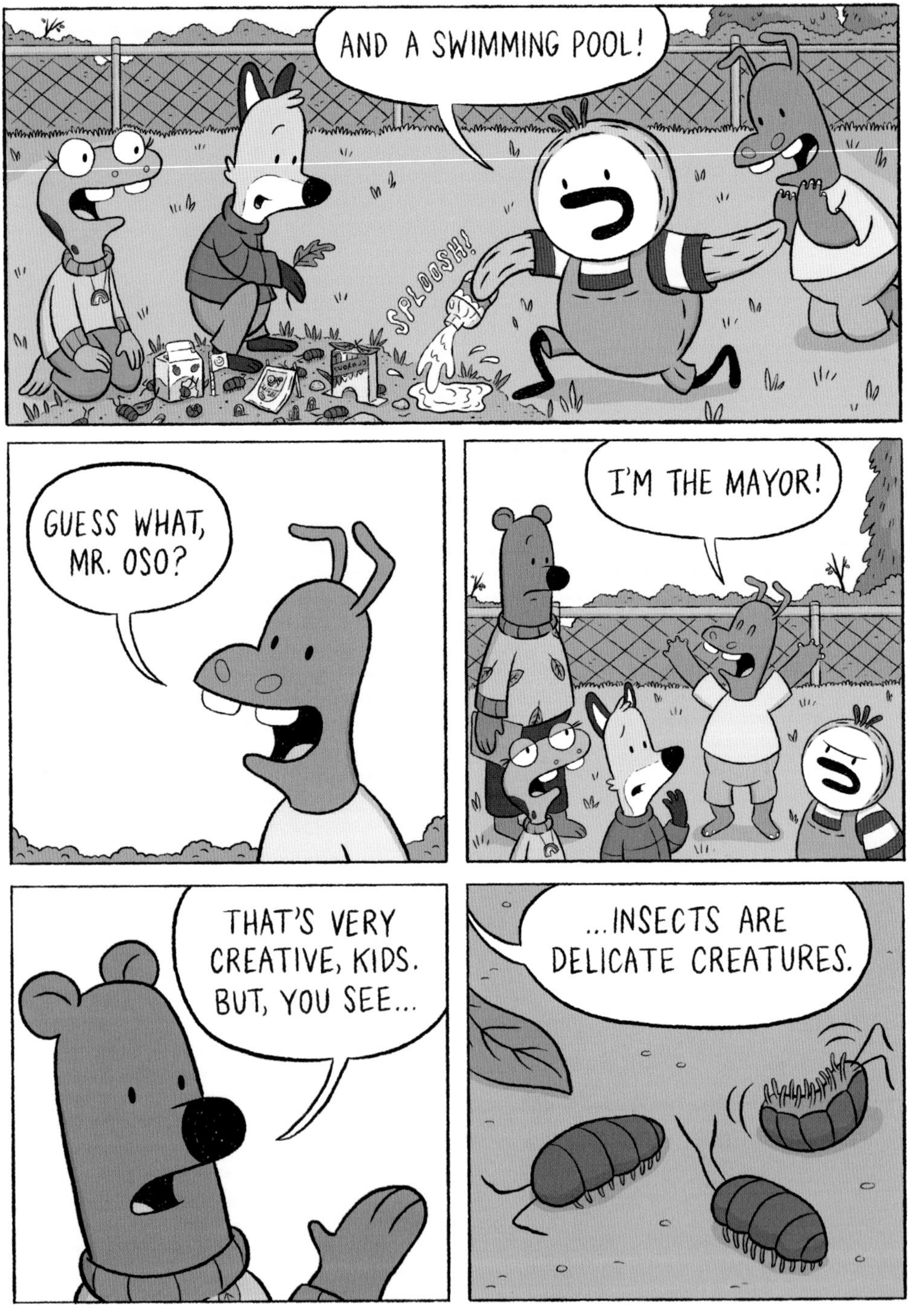
AND A SWIMMING POOL!
SPLOOSH!
GUESS WHAT, MR. OSO?
I'M THE MAYOR!
THAT'S VERY CREATIVE, KIDS. BUT, YOU SEE...
...INSECTS ARE DELICATE CREATURES.

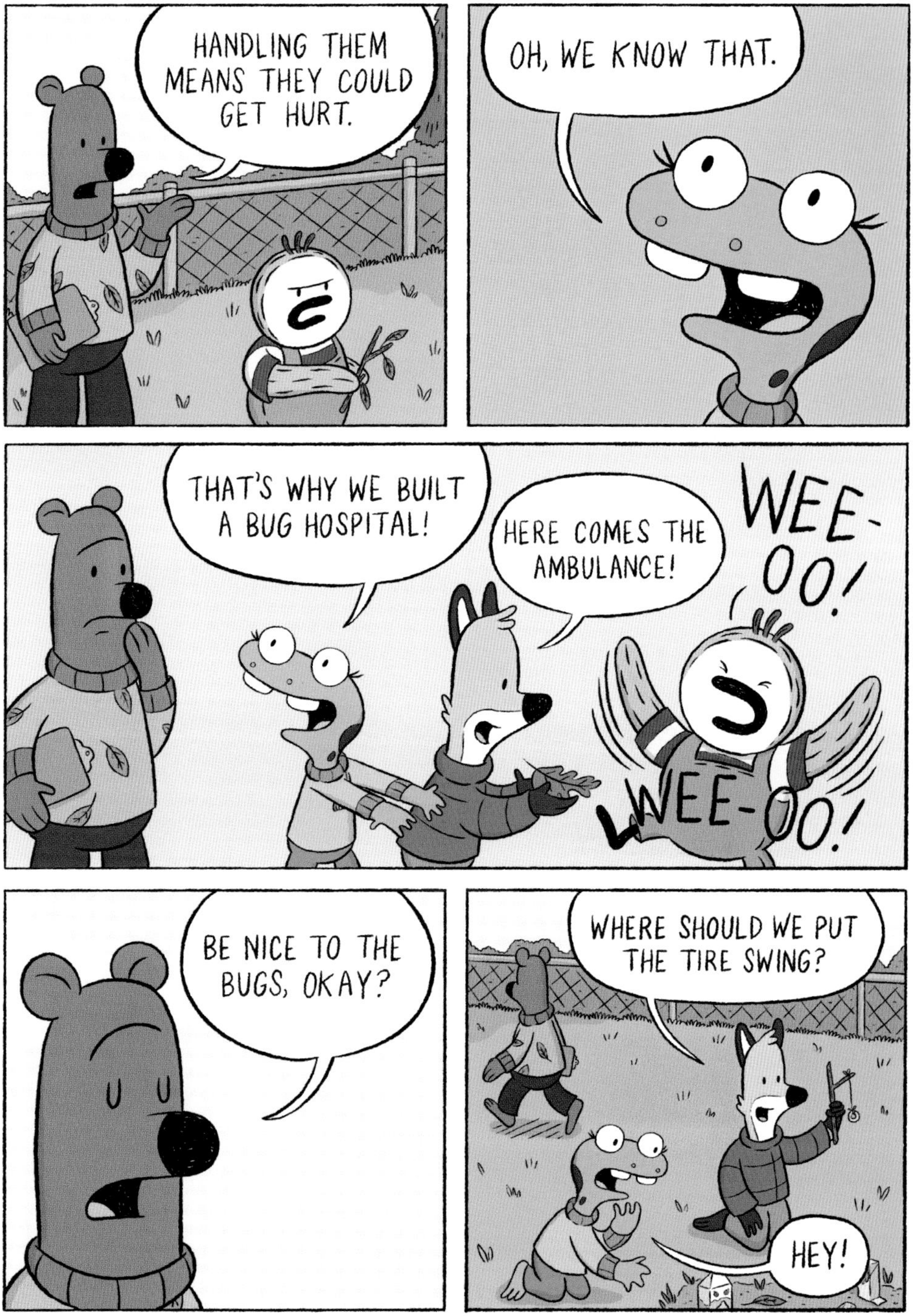
HANDLING THEM MEANS THEY COULD GET HURT.
OH, WE KNOW THAT.
THAT'S WHY WE BUILT A BUG HOSPITAL!
HERE COMES THE AMBULANCE!
WEE-OO!
WEE-OO!
BE NICE TO THE BUGS, OKAY?
WHERE SHOULD WE PUT THE TIRE SWING?
HEY!

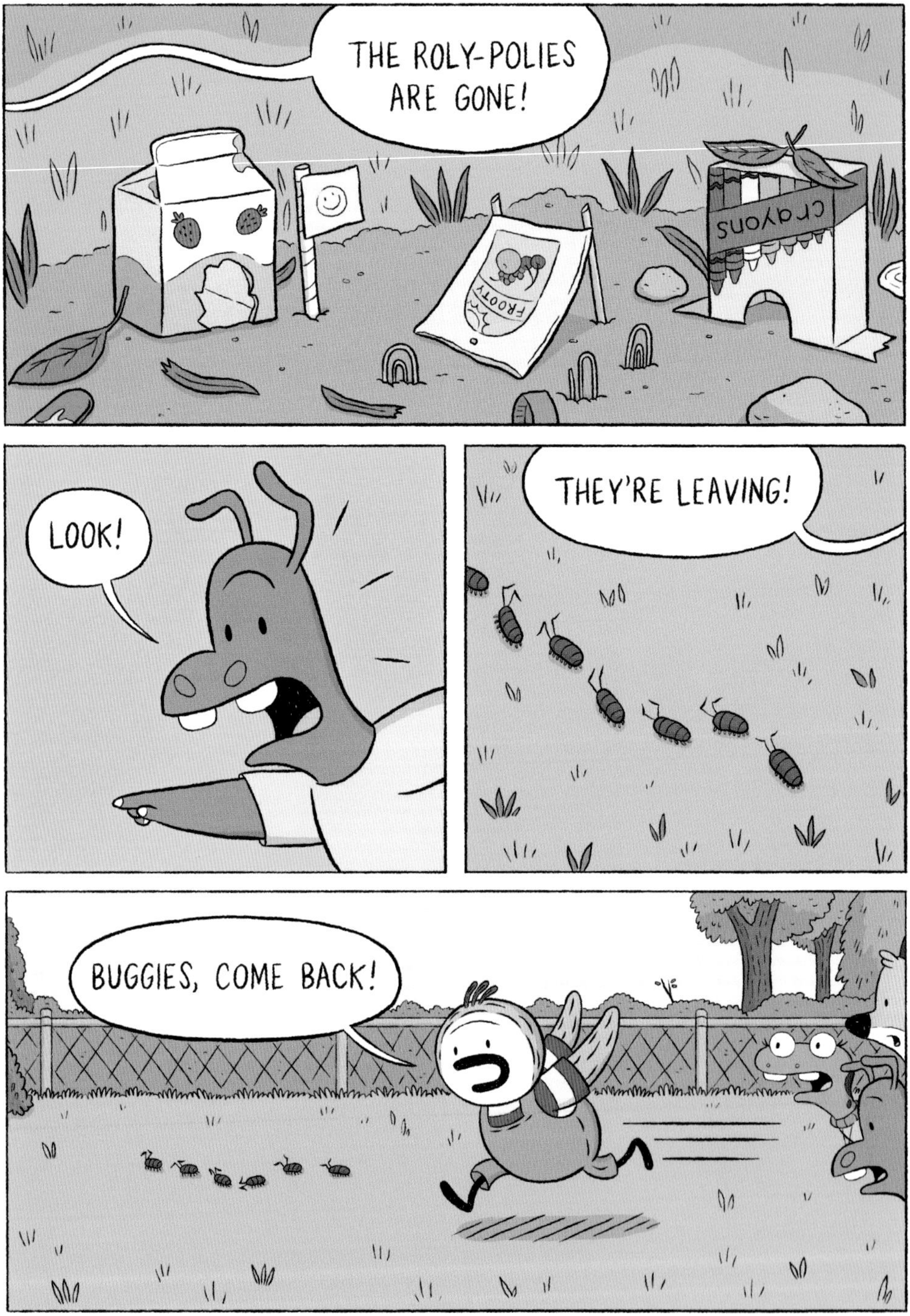
THE ROLY-POLIES ARE GONE!
crayons
FROOTY
LOOK!
THEY'RE LEAVING!
BUGGIES, COME BACK!

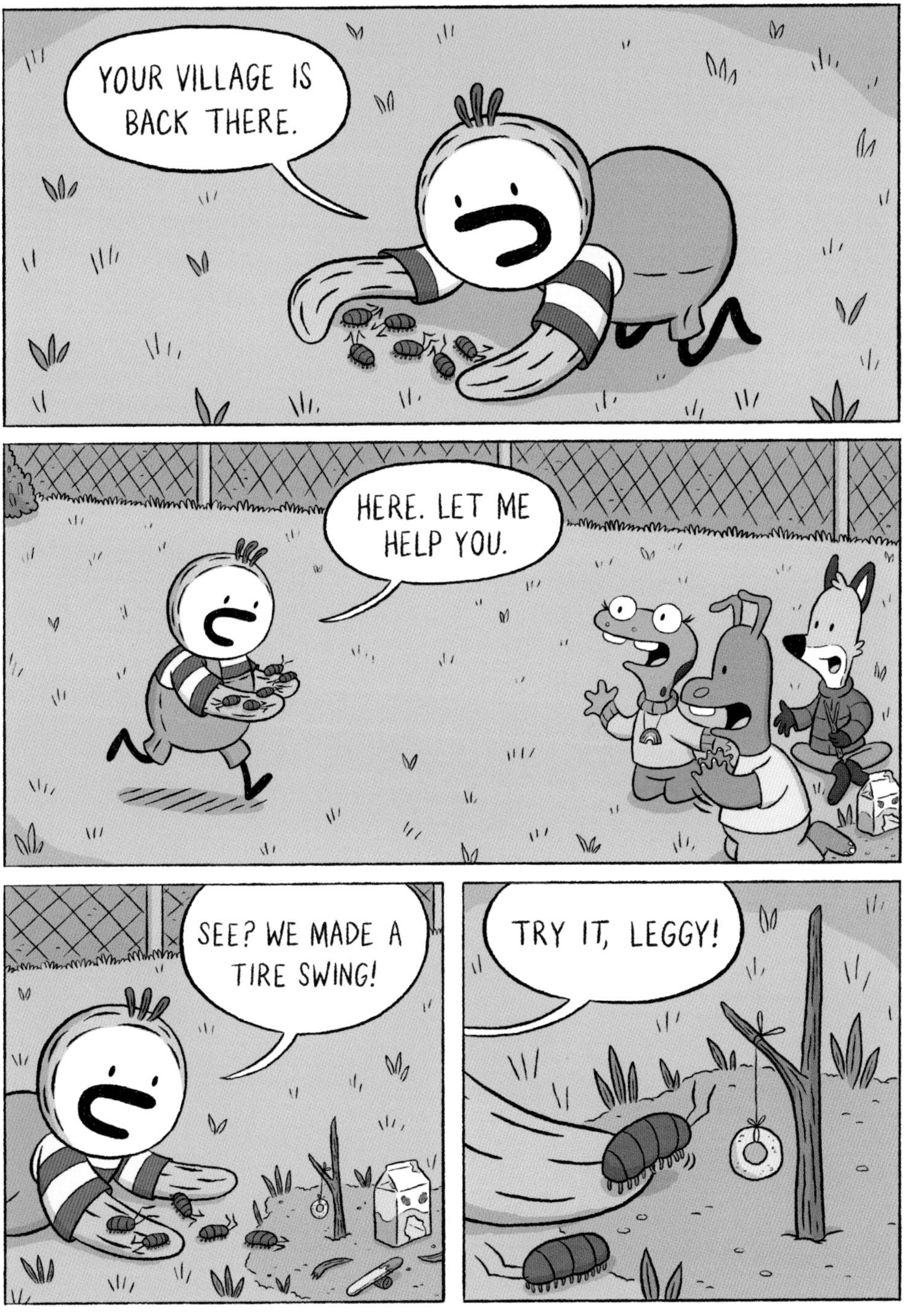
YOUR VILLAGE IS BACK THERE.
HERE. LET ME HELP YOU.
SEE? WE MADE A TIRE SWING!
TRY IT, LEGGY!

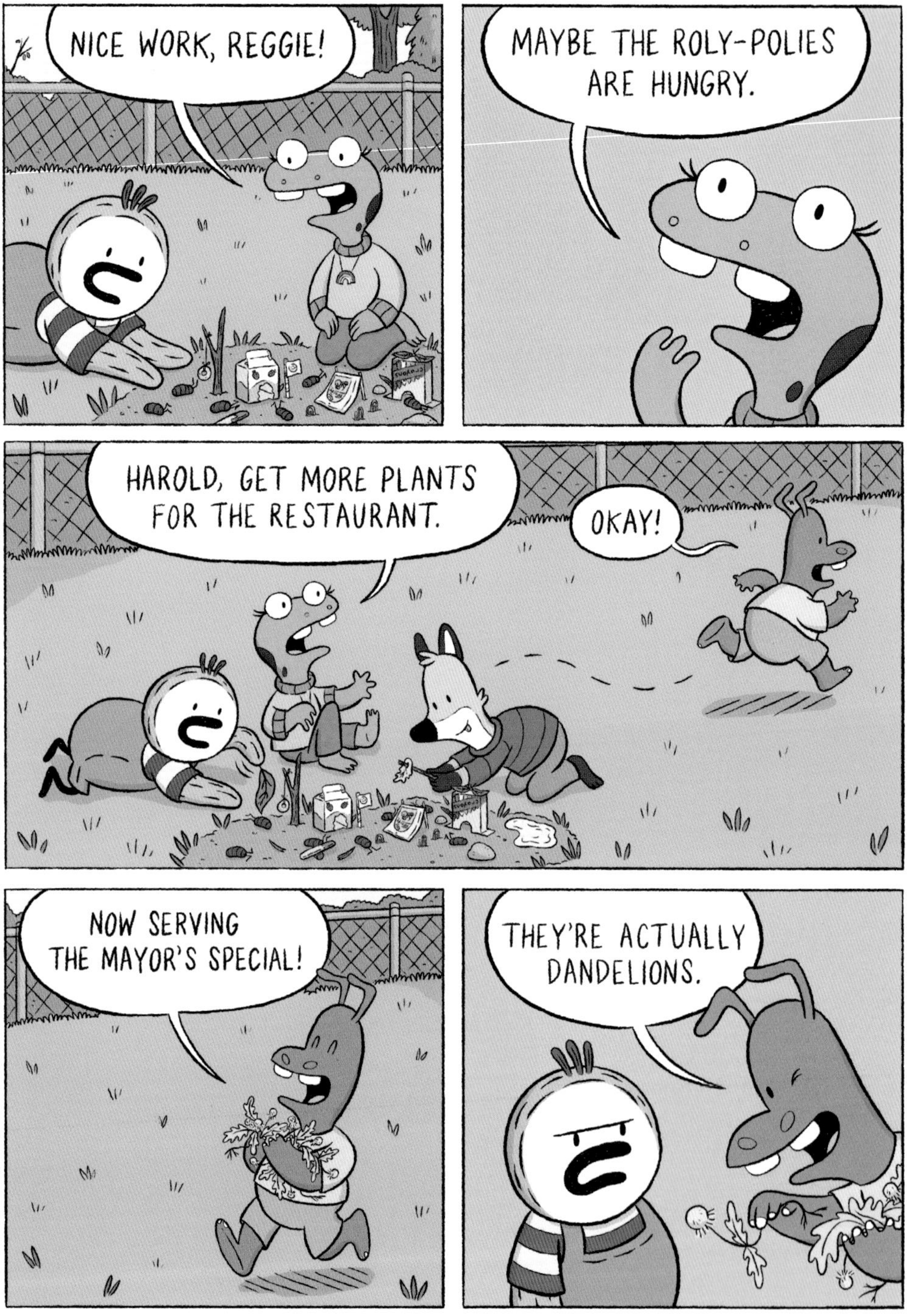
NICE WORK, REGGIE!
MAYBE THE ROLY-POLIES ARE HUNGRY.
HAROLD, GET MORE PLANTS FOR THE RESTAURANT.
OKAY!
NOW SERVING THE MAYOR'S SPECIAL!
THEY'RE ACTUALLY DANDELIONS.

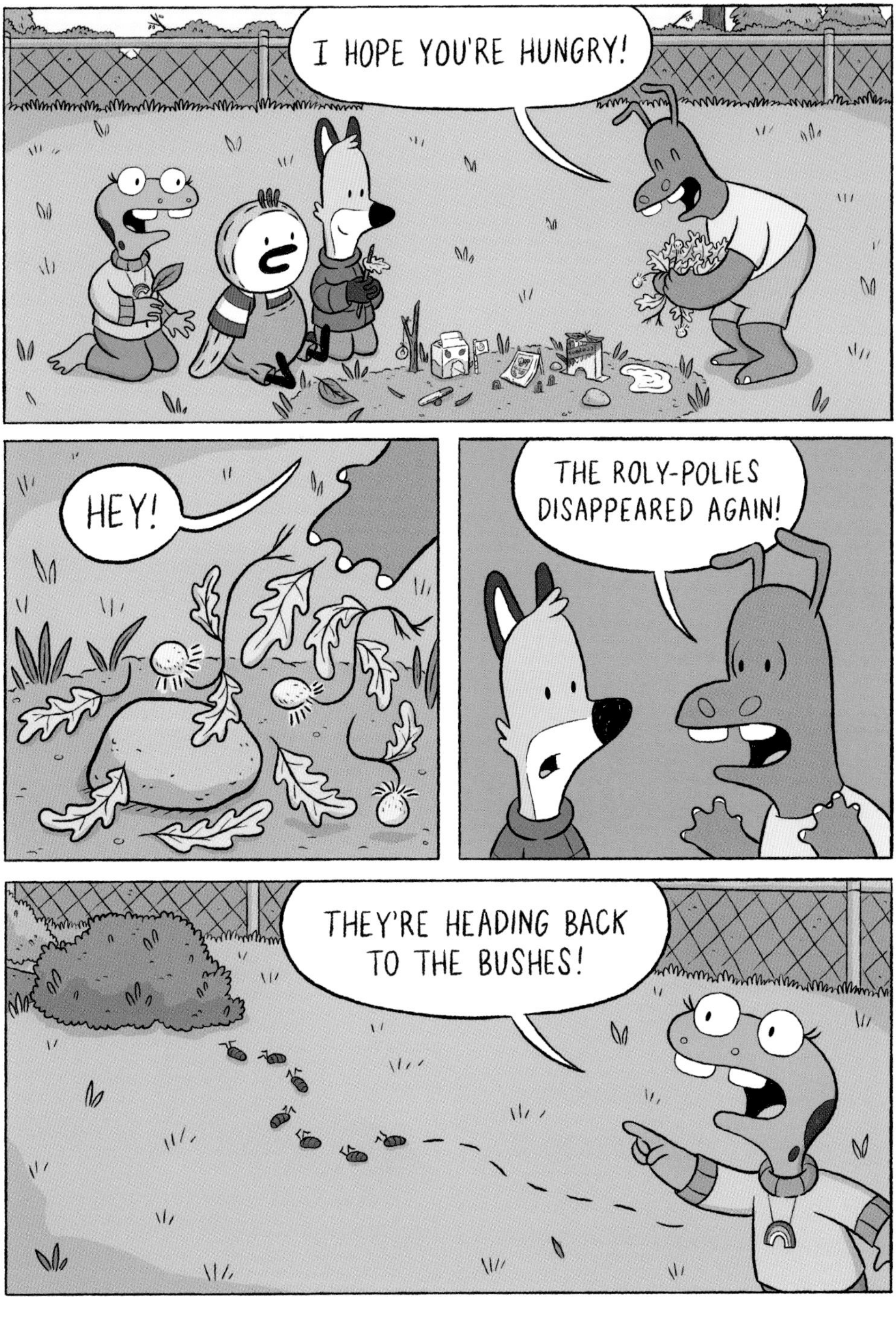
I HOPE YOU'RE HUNGRY!
HEY!
THE ROLY-POLIES DISAPPEARED AGAIN!
THEY'RE HEADING BACK TO THE BUSHES!

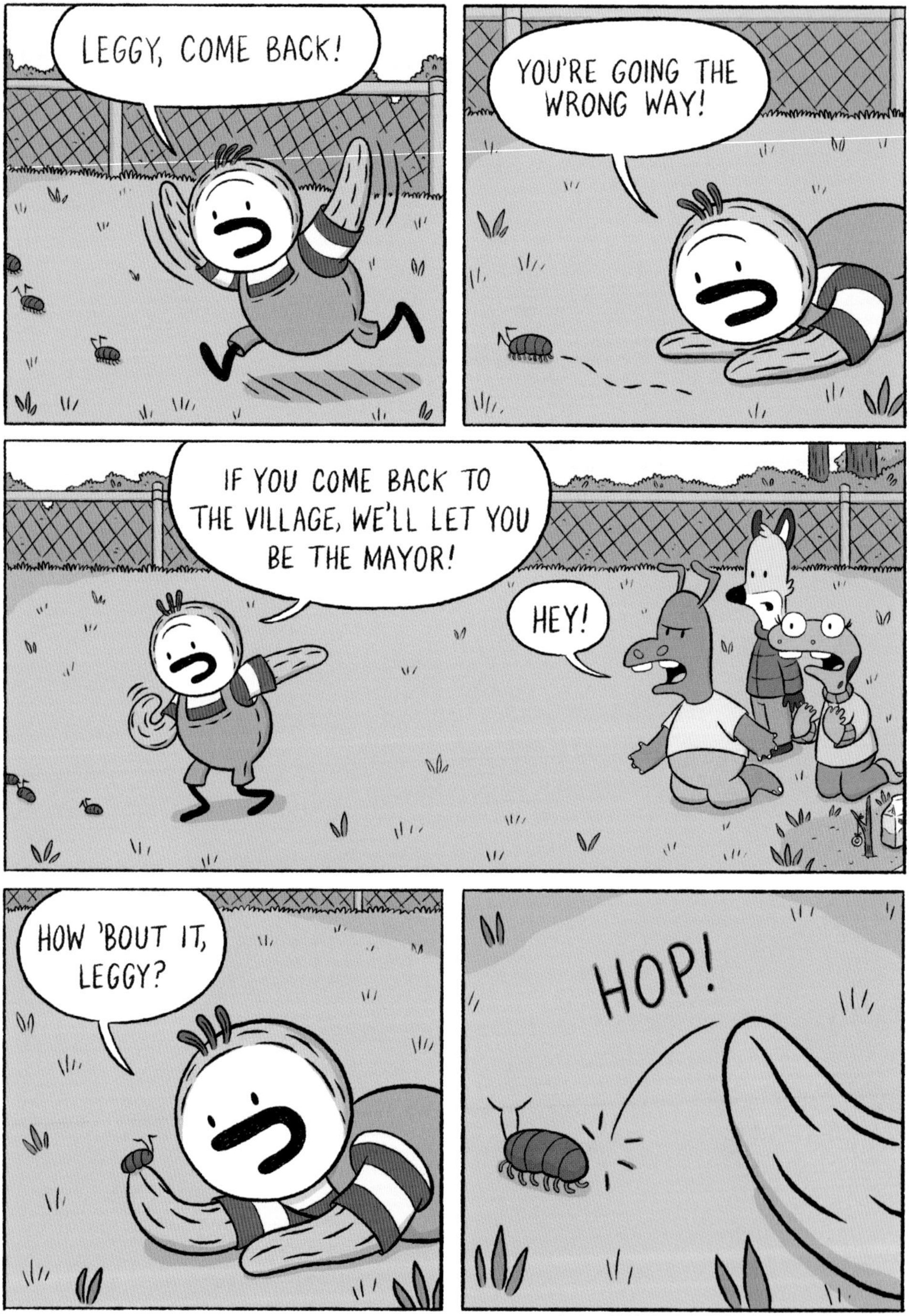
LEGGY, COME BACK!
YOU'RE GOING THE WRONG WAY!
IF YOU COME BACK TO THE VILLAGE, WE'LL LET YOU BE THE MAYOR!
HEY!
HOW 'BOUT IT, LEGGY?
HOP!

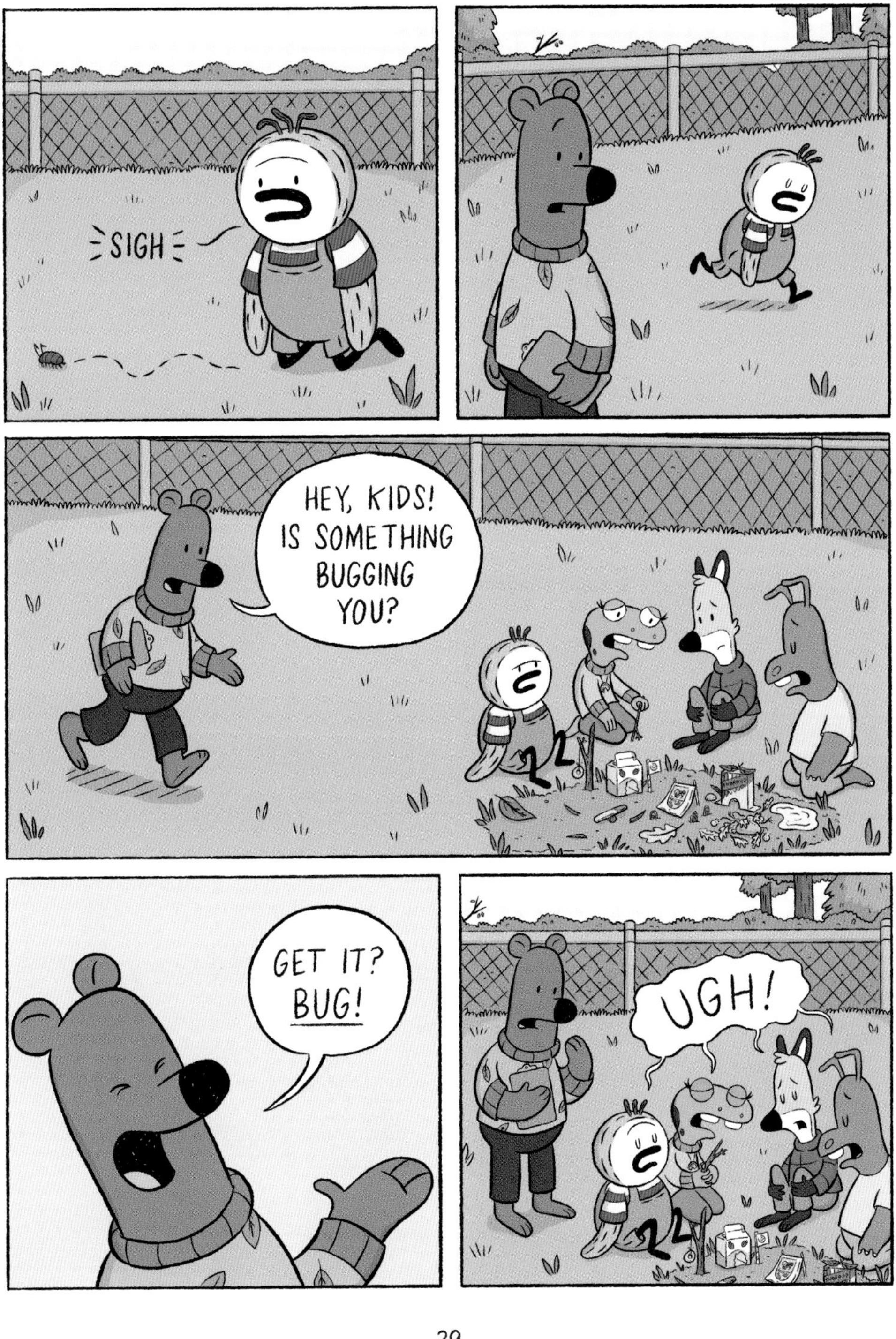
SIGH
HEY, KIDS! IS SOMETHING BUGGING YOU?
GET IT? BUG!
UGH!

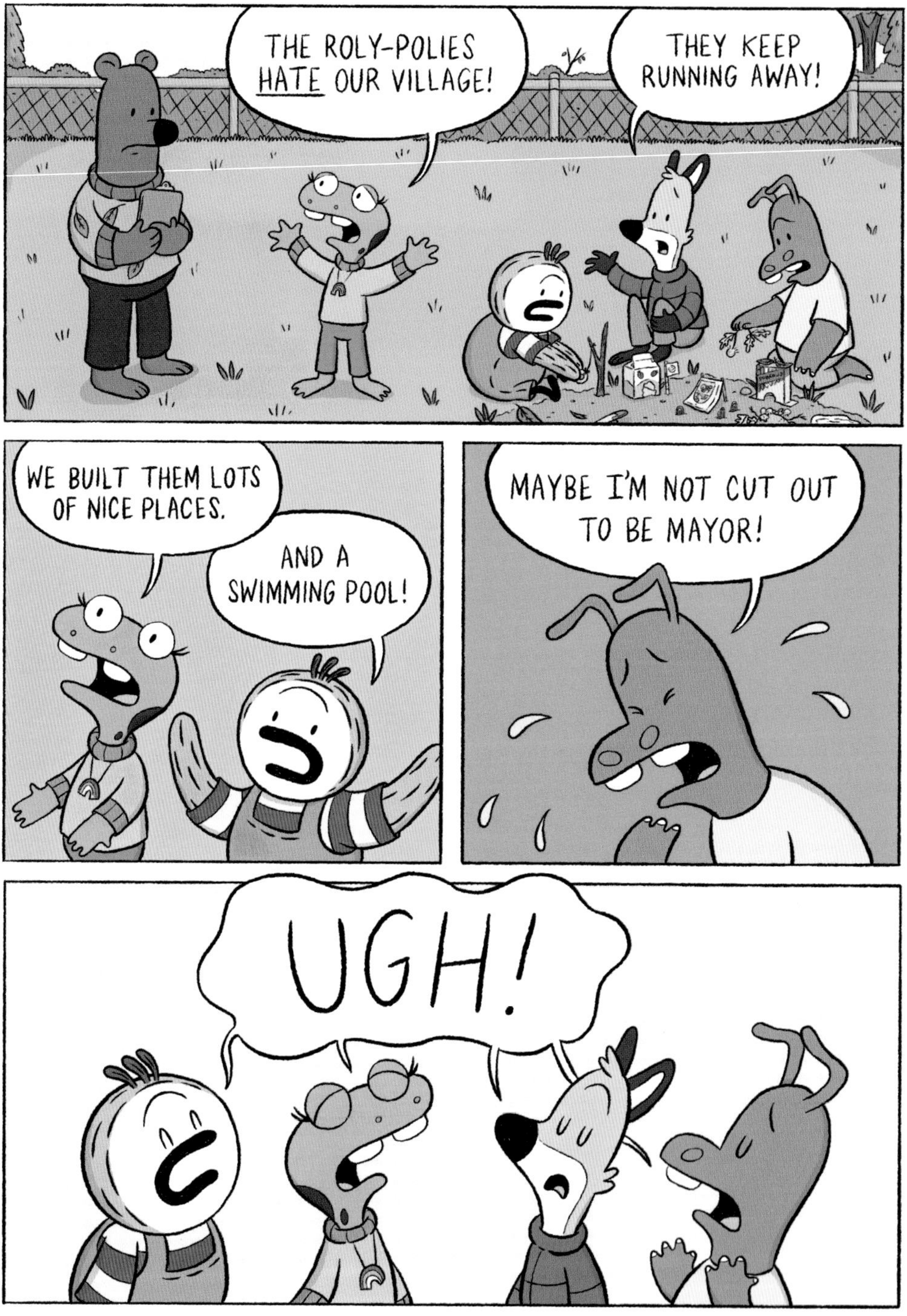
THE ROLY-POLIES HATE OUR VILLAGE!
THEY KEEP RUNNING AWAY!
WE BUILT THEM LOTS OF NICE PLACES.
AND A SWIMMING POOL!
MAYBE I'M NOT CUT OUT TO BE MAYOR!
UGH!

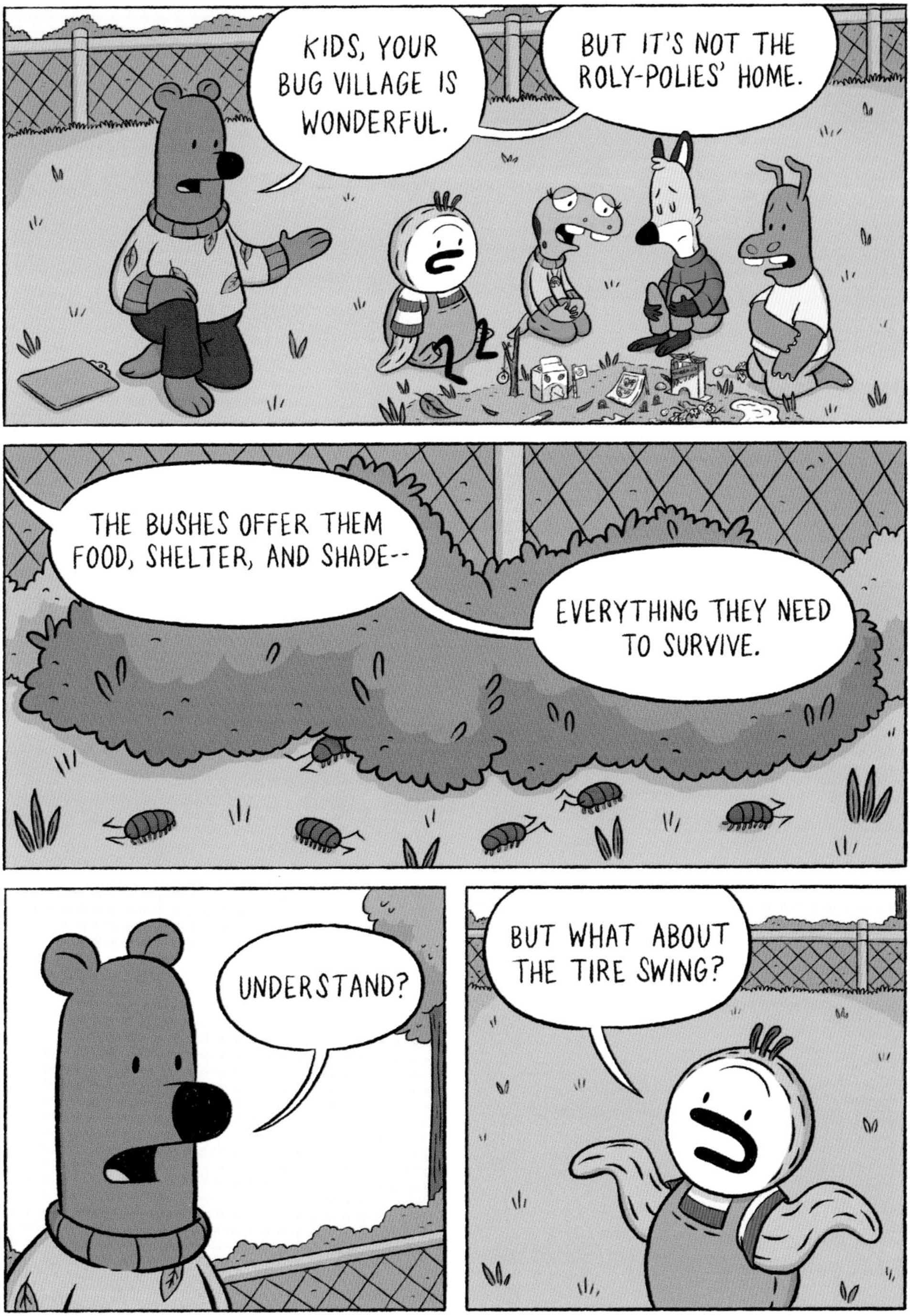

KIDS, YOUR BUG VILLAGE IS WONDERFUL.
BUT IT'S NOT THE ROLY-POLIES' HOME.
THE BUSHES OFFER THEM FOOD, SHELTER, AND SHADE--
EVERYTHING THEY NEED TO SURVIVE.
UNDERSTAND?
BUT WHAT ABOUT THE TIRE SWING?

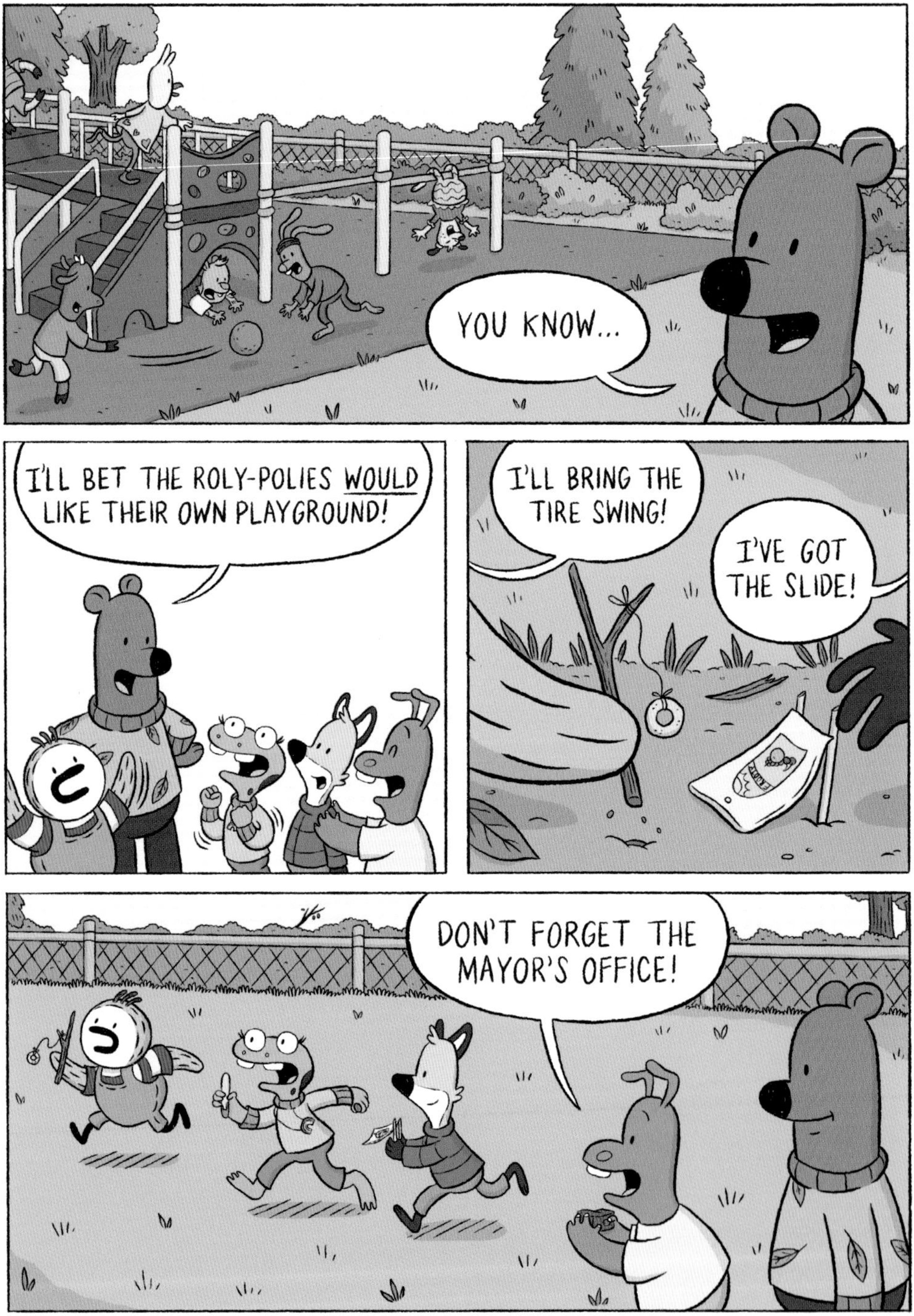
YOU KNOW...
I'LL BET THE ROLY-POLIES WOULD LIKE THEIR OWN PLAYGROUND!
I'LL BRING THE TIRE SWING!
I'VE GOT THE SLIDE!
DON'T FORGET THE MAYOR'S OFFICE!

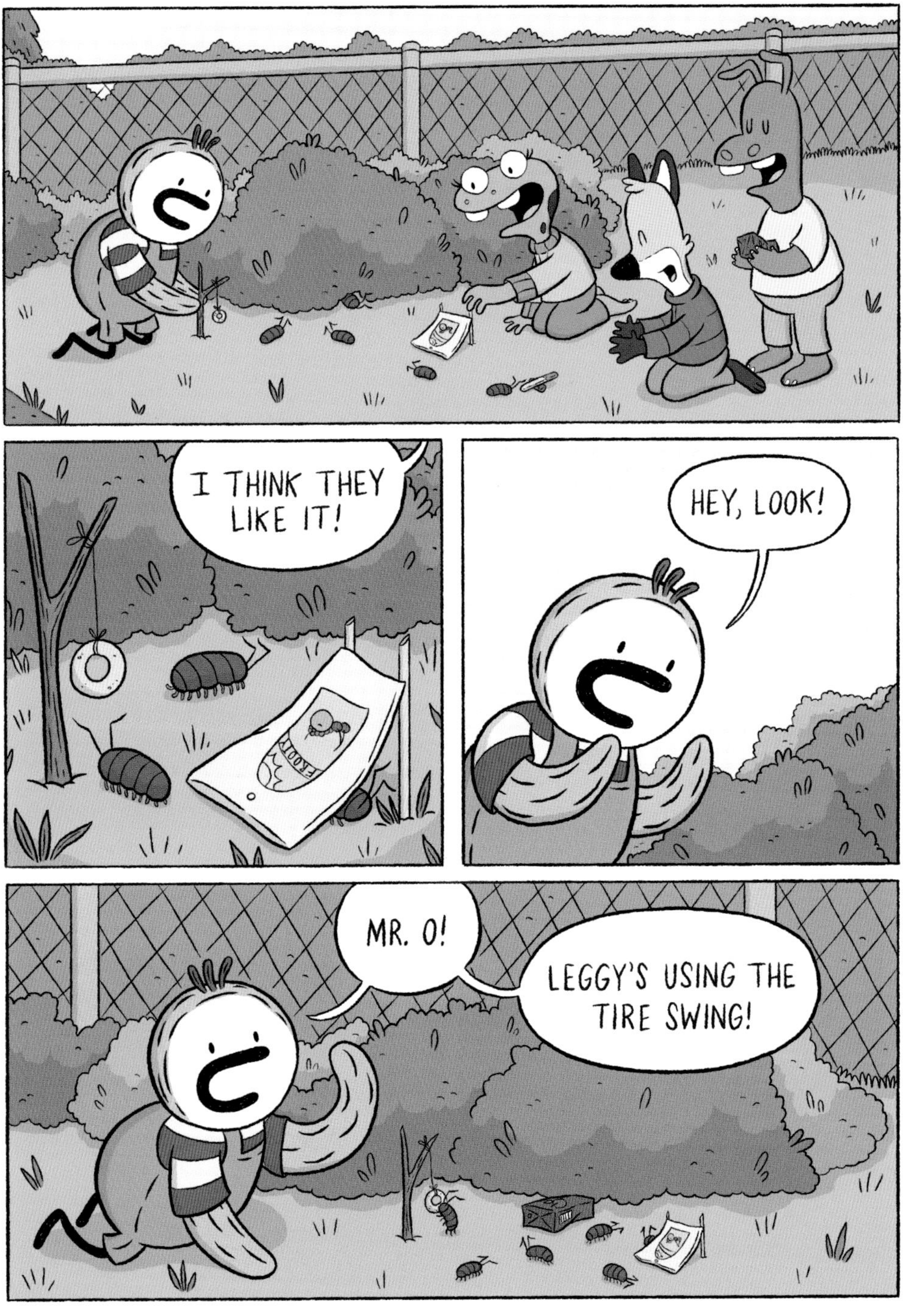
I THINK THEY LIKE IT!
HEY, LOOK!
MR. O!
LEGGY'S USING THE TIRE SWING!

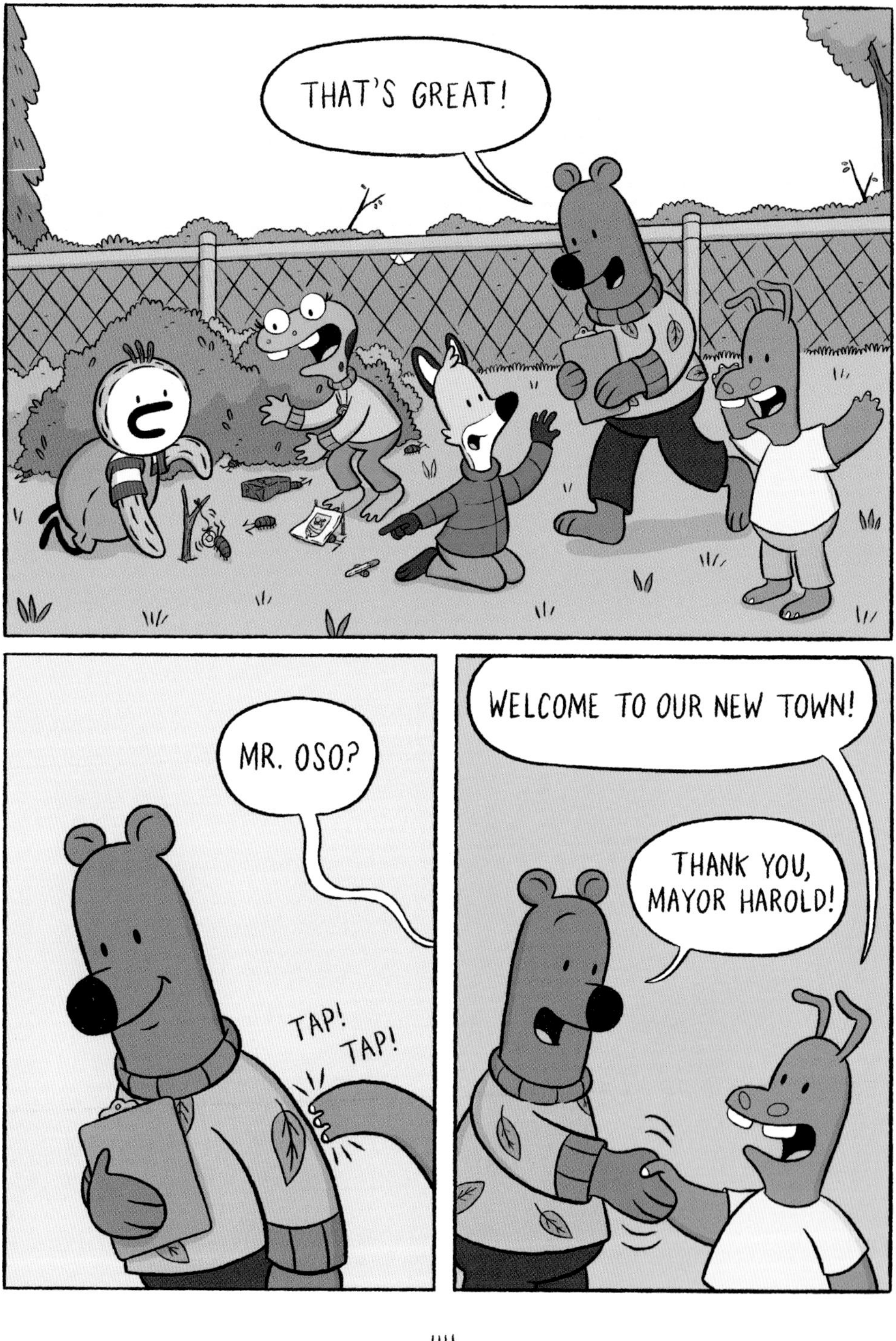
THAT'S GREAT!
MR. OSO?
TAP!
TAP!
WELCOME TO OUR NEW TOWN!
THANK YOU, MAYOR HAROLD!

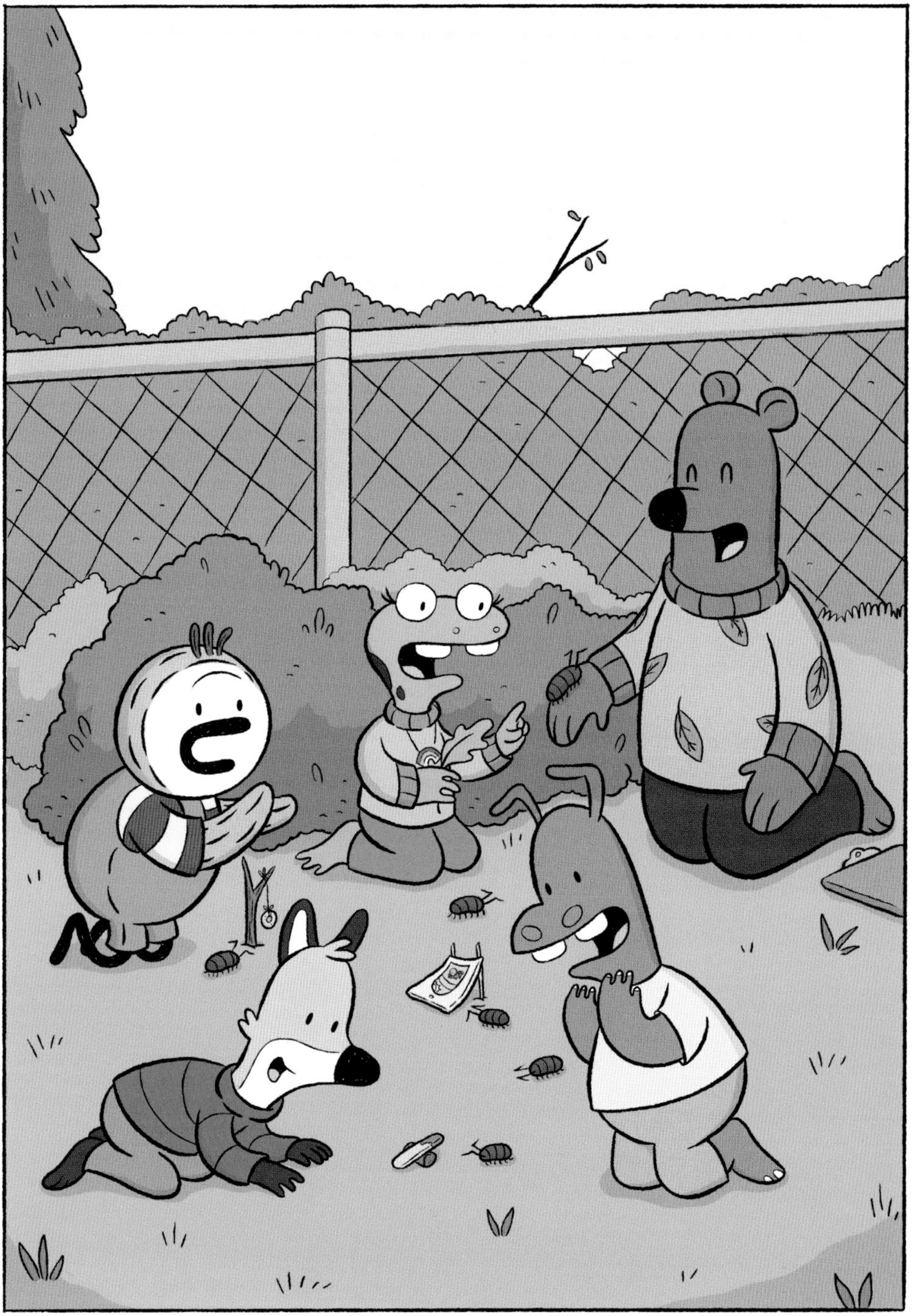

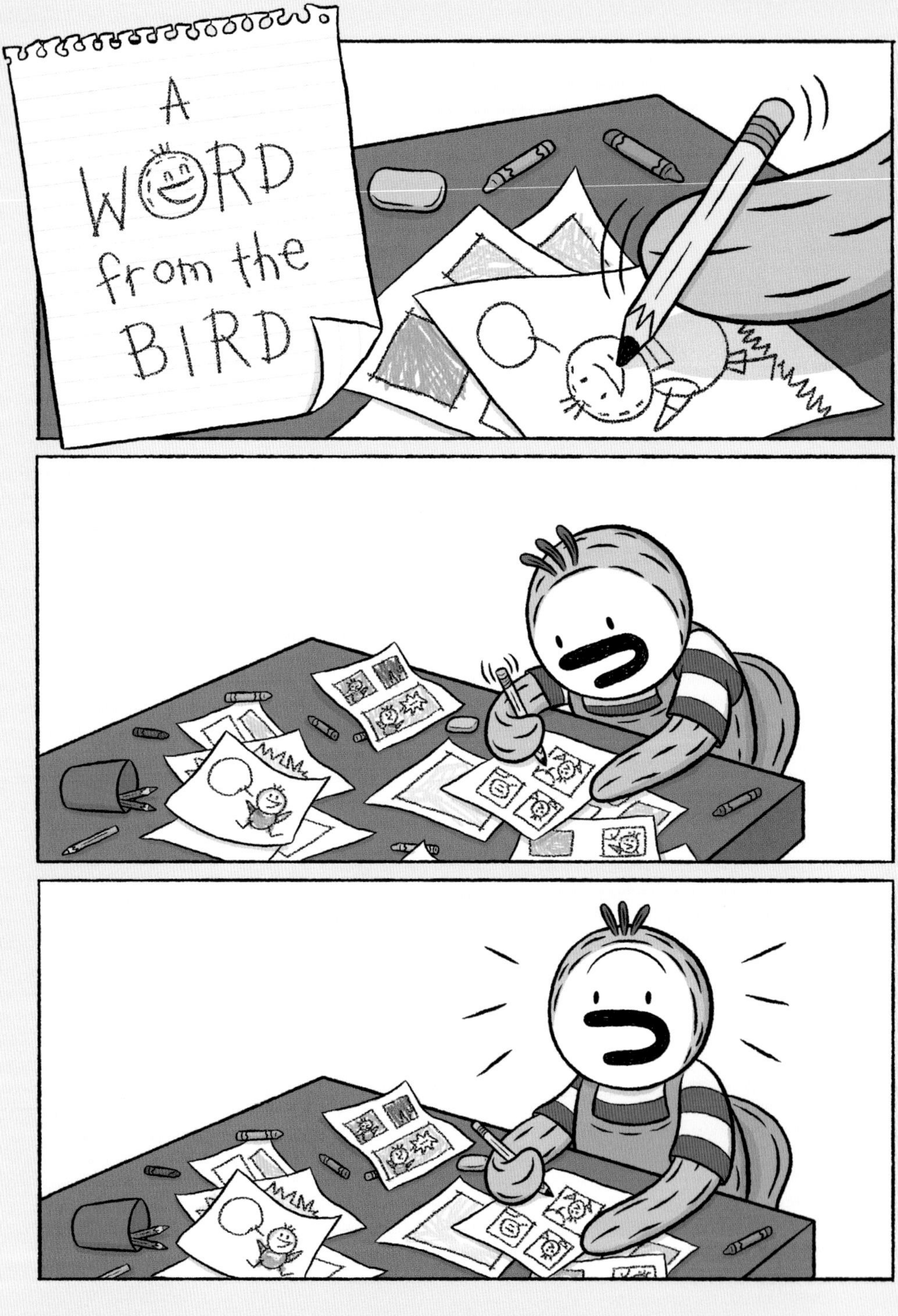
A WORD from the BIRD

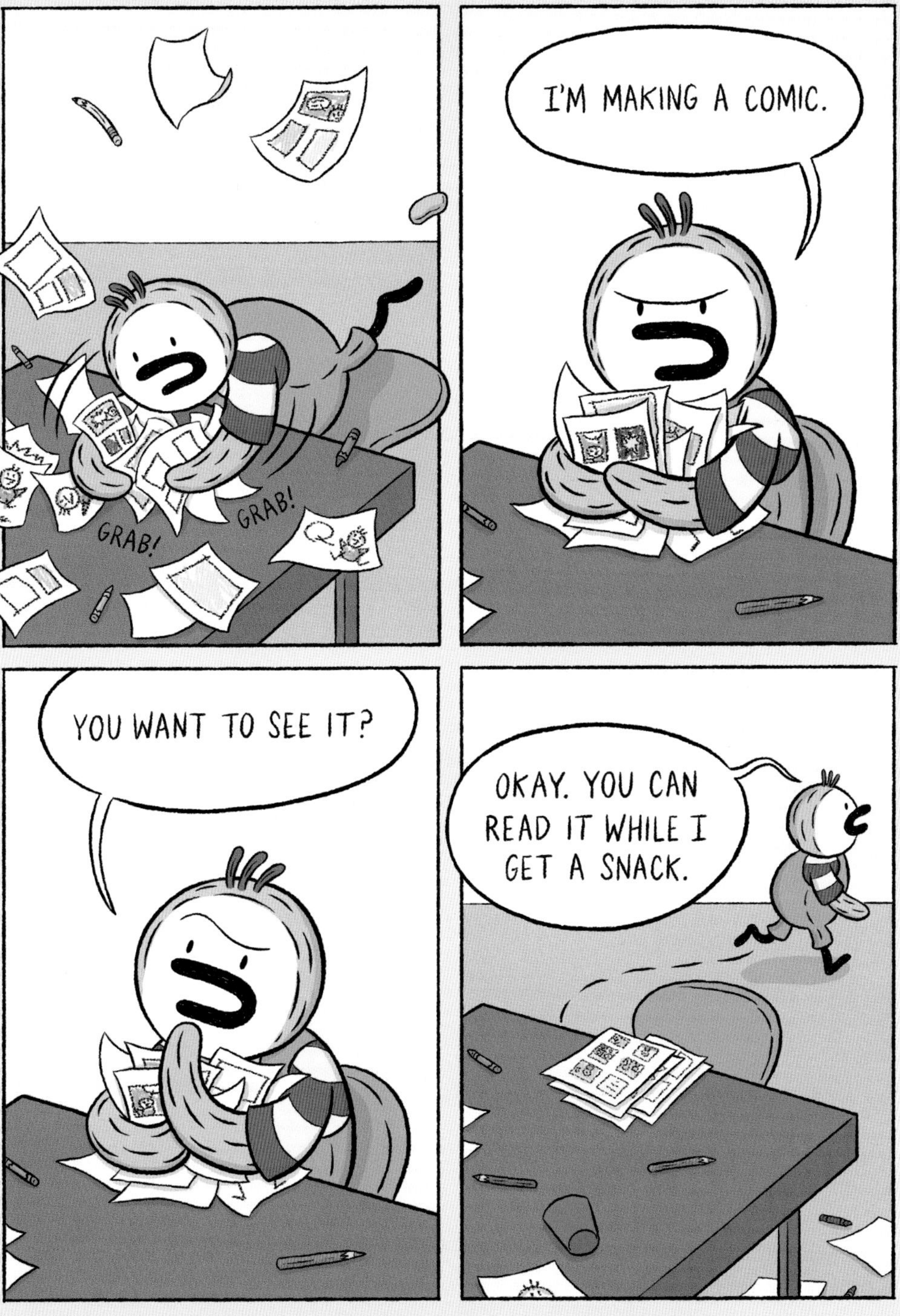
GRAB!
GRAB!
I'M MAKING A COMIC.
YOU WANT TO SEE IT?
OKAY. YOU CAN READ IT WHILE I GET A SNACK.

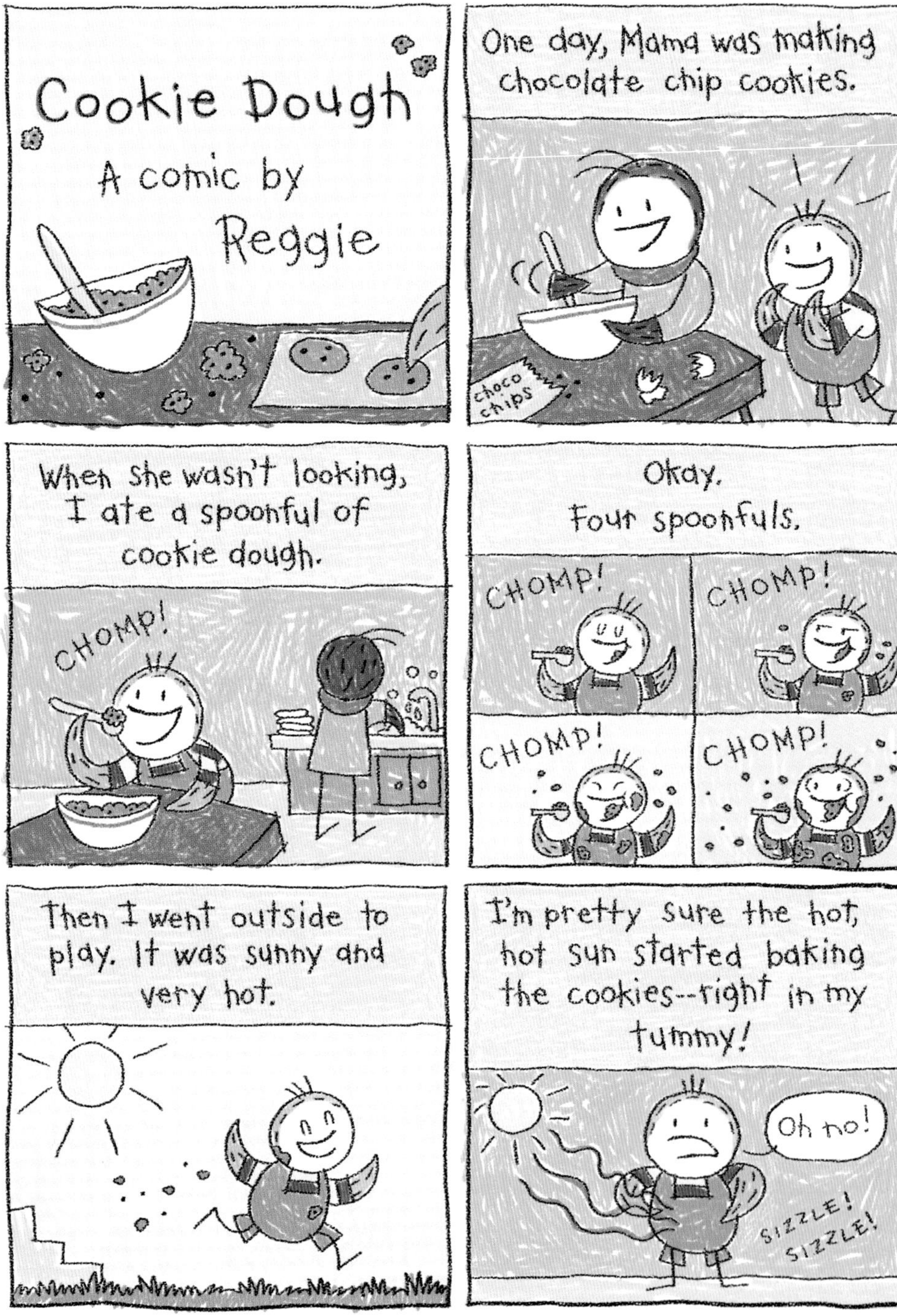
Cookie Dough
A comic by
Reggie
One day, Mama was making chocolate chip cookies.
choco chips
When she wasn't looking, I ate a spoonful of cookie dough.
CHOMP!
Okay. Four spoonfuls.
CHOMP!
CHOMP!
CHOMP!
CHOMP!
Then I went outside to play. It was sunny and very hot.
I'm pretty sure the hot, hot sun started baking the cookies--right in my tummy!
Oh no!
SIZZLE! SIZZLE!

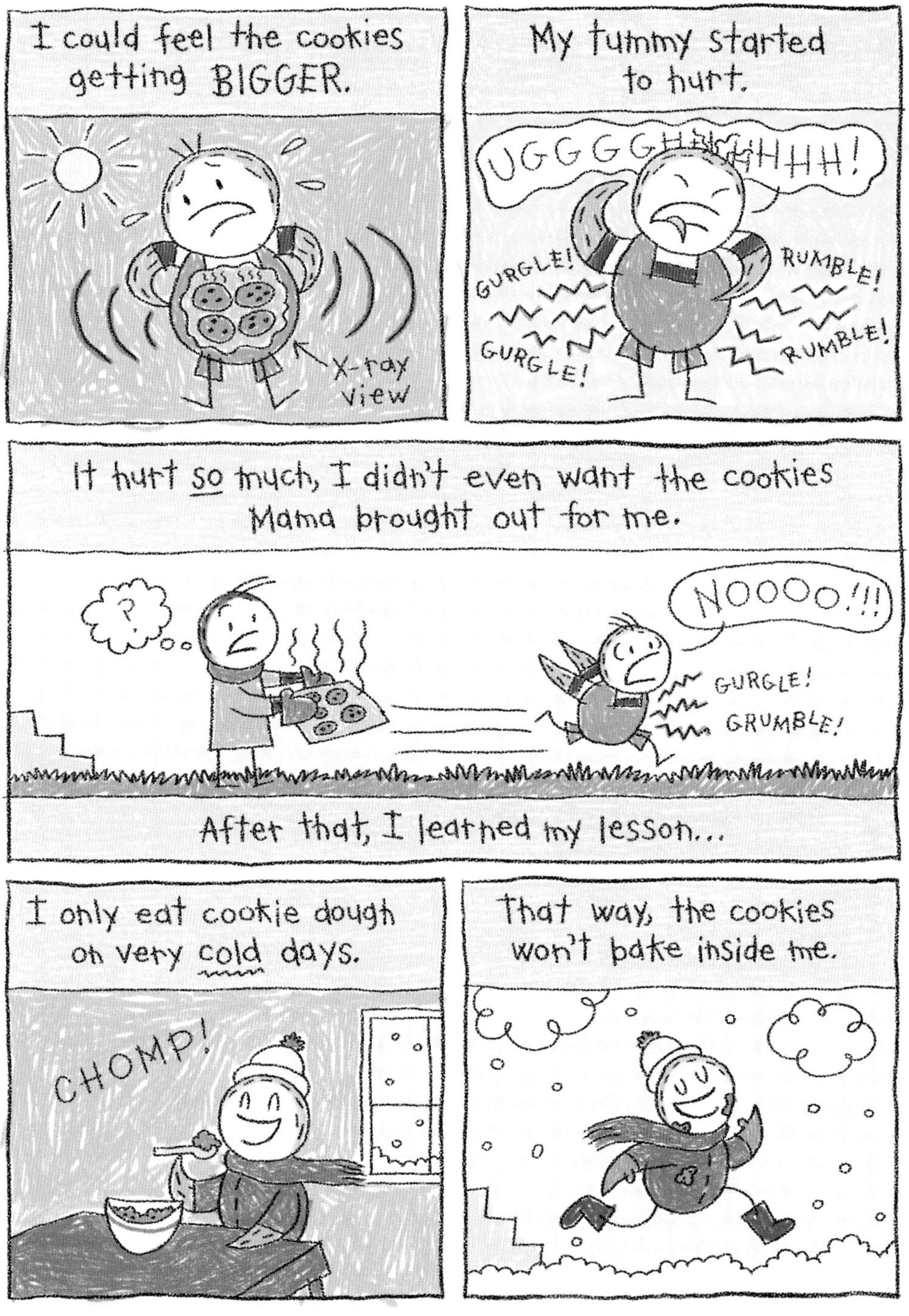
I could feel the cookies getting BIGGER.
X-ray view
My tummy started to hurt.
UGGGGHHHHHH!
GURGLE!
GURGLE!
RUMBLE!
RUMBLE!
It hurt so much, I didn't even want the cookies Mama brought out for me.
?
NOOOO!!!
GURGLE!
GRUMBLE!
After that, I learned my lesson...
I only eat cookie dough on very cold days.
CHOMP!
That way, the cookies won't bake inside me.

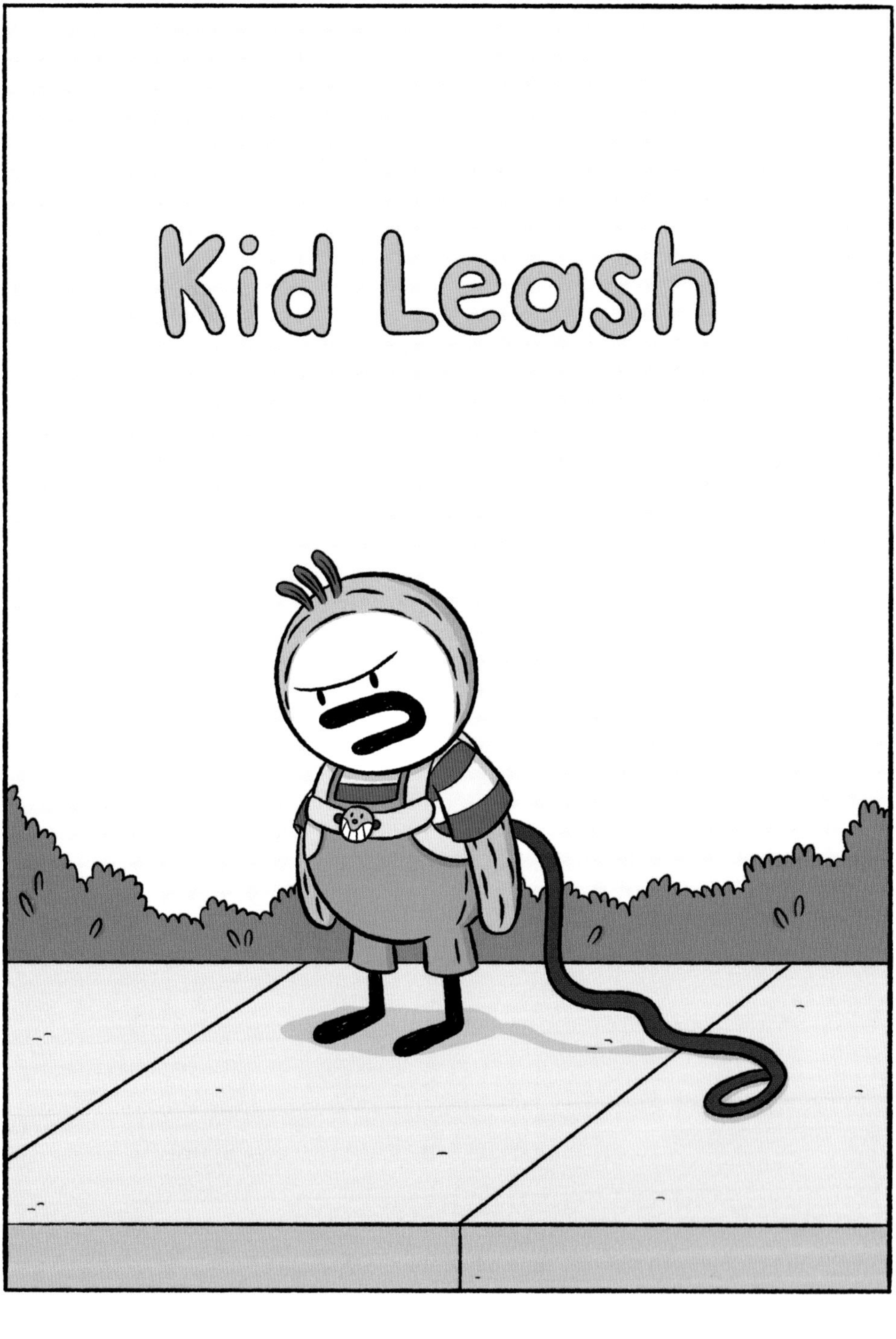
Kid Leash

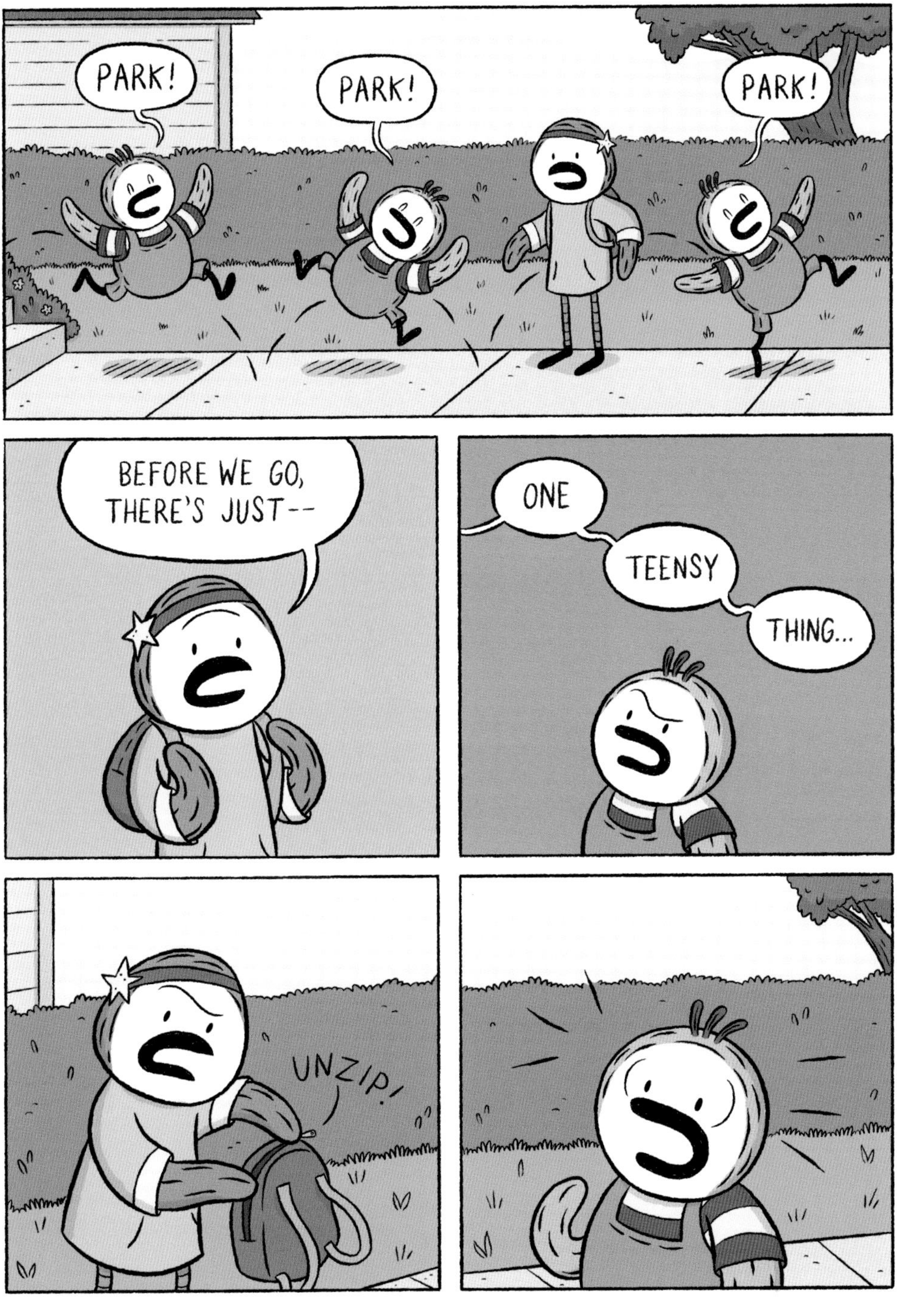
PARK!
PARK!
PARK!
BEFORE WE GO, THERE'S JUST--
ONE
TEENSY
THING...
UNZIP!

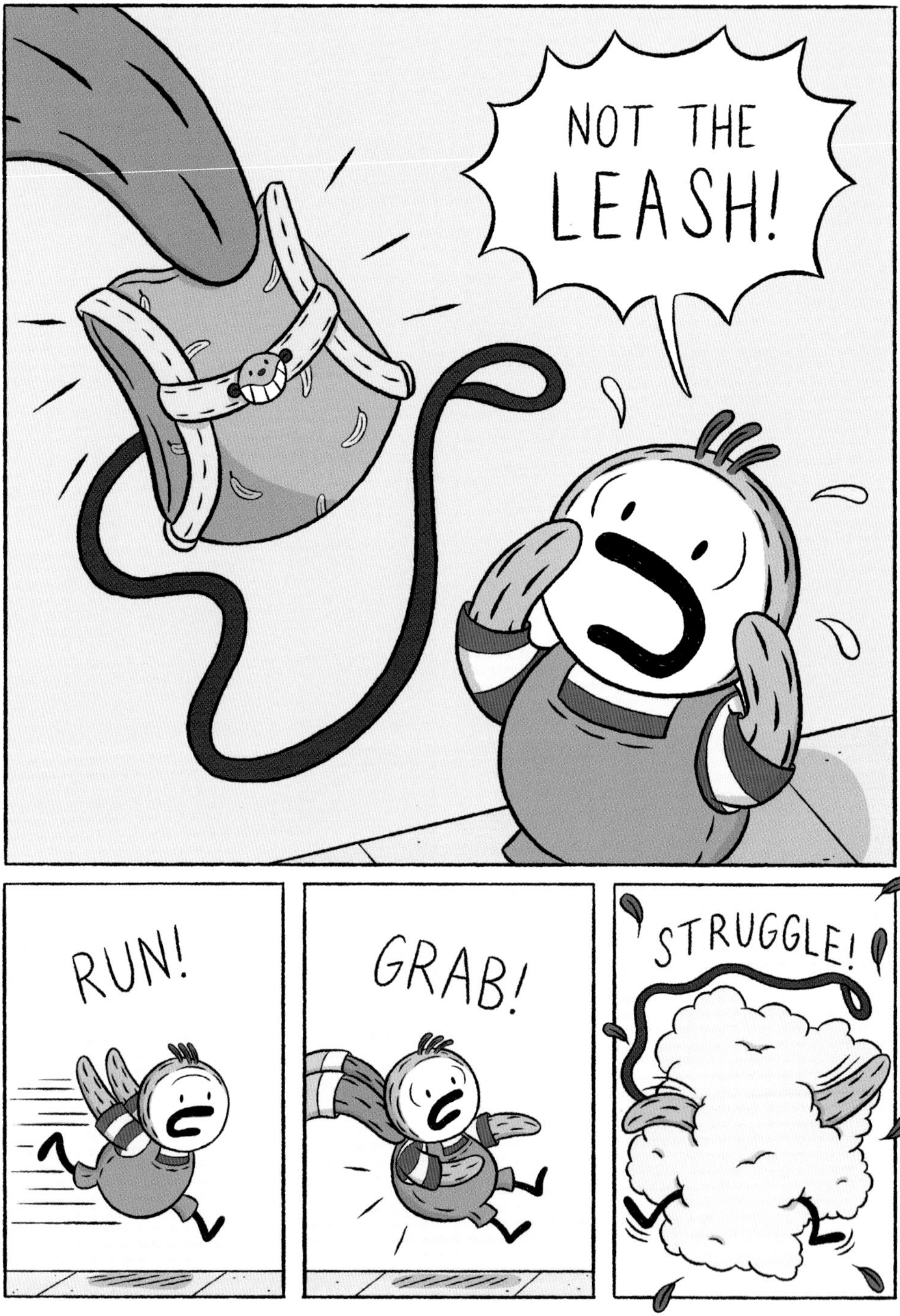
NOT THE LEASH!
RUN!
GRAB!
STRUGGLE!

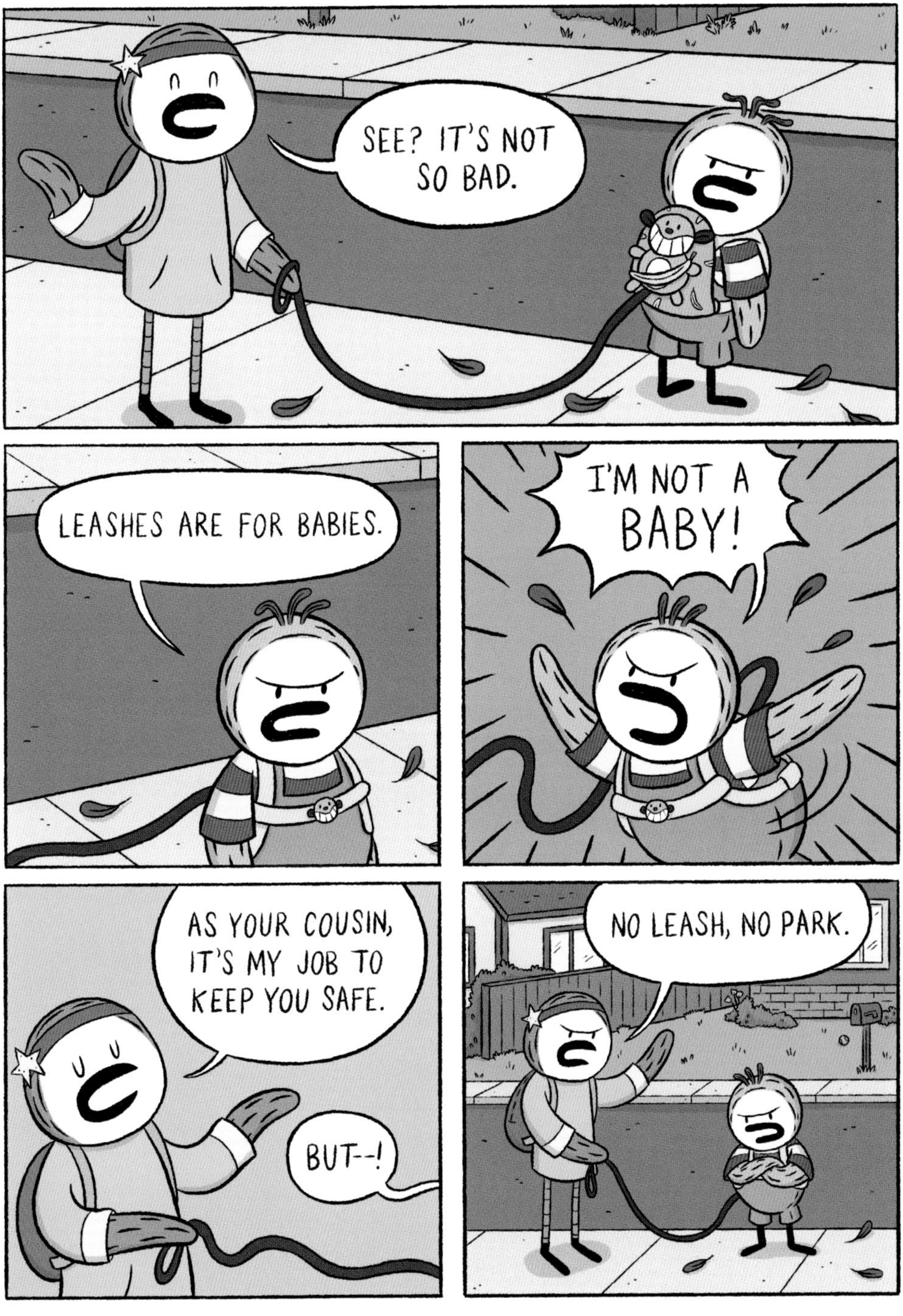
SEE? IT'S NOT SO BAD.
LEASHES ARE FOR BABIES.
I'M NOT A BABY!
AS YOUR COUSIN, IT'S MY JOB TO KEEP YOU SAFE.
BUT--!
NO LEASH, NO PARK.

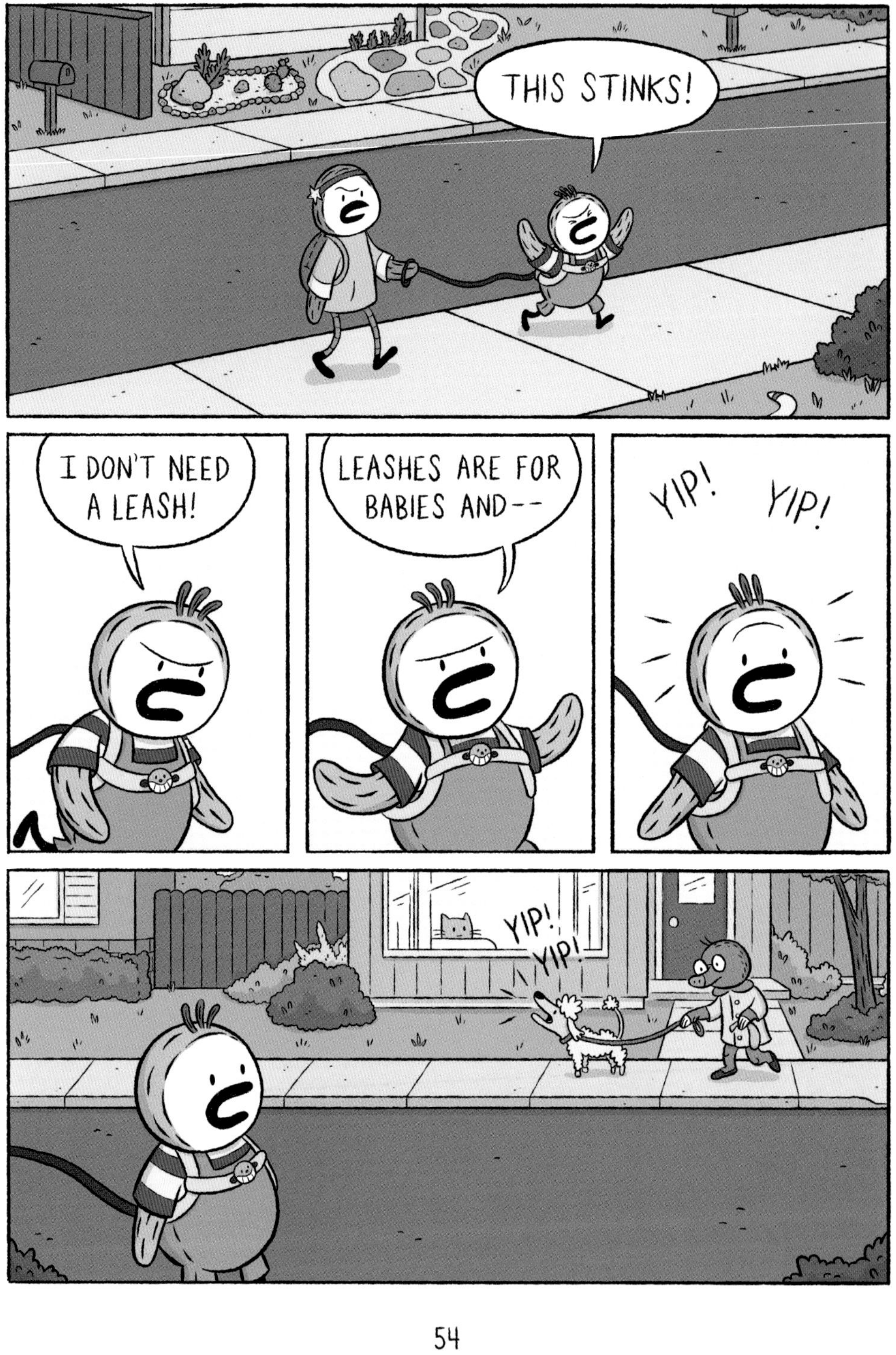
THIS STINKS!
I DON'T NEED A LEASH!
LEASHES ARE FOR BABIES AND--
YIP! YIP!
YIP! YIP!

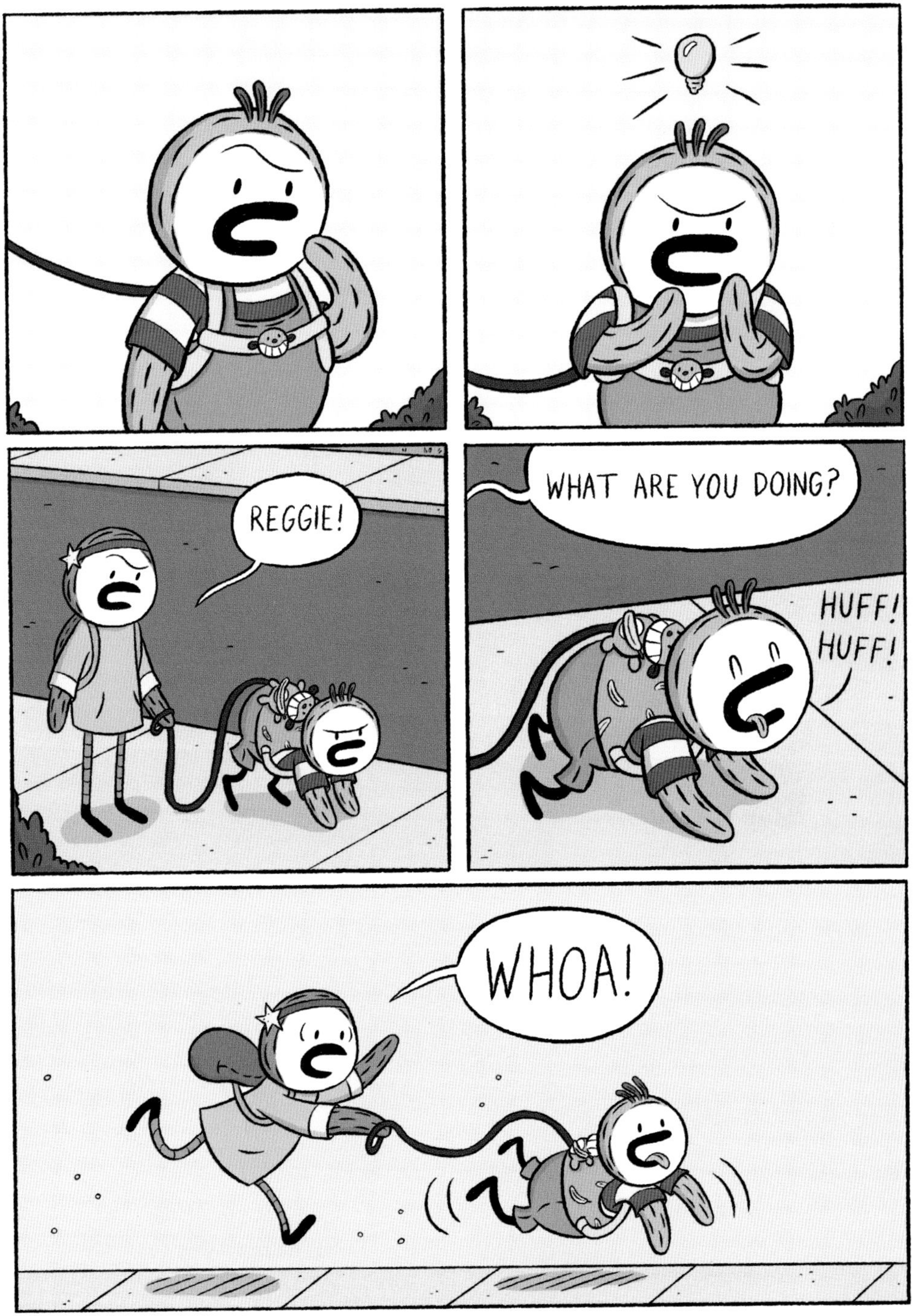
REGGIE!
WHAT ARE YOU DOING?
HUFF! HUFF!
WHOA!

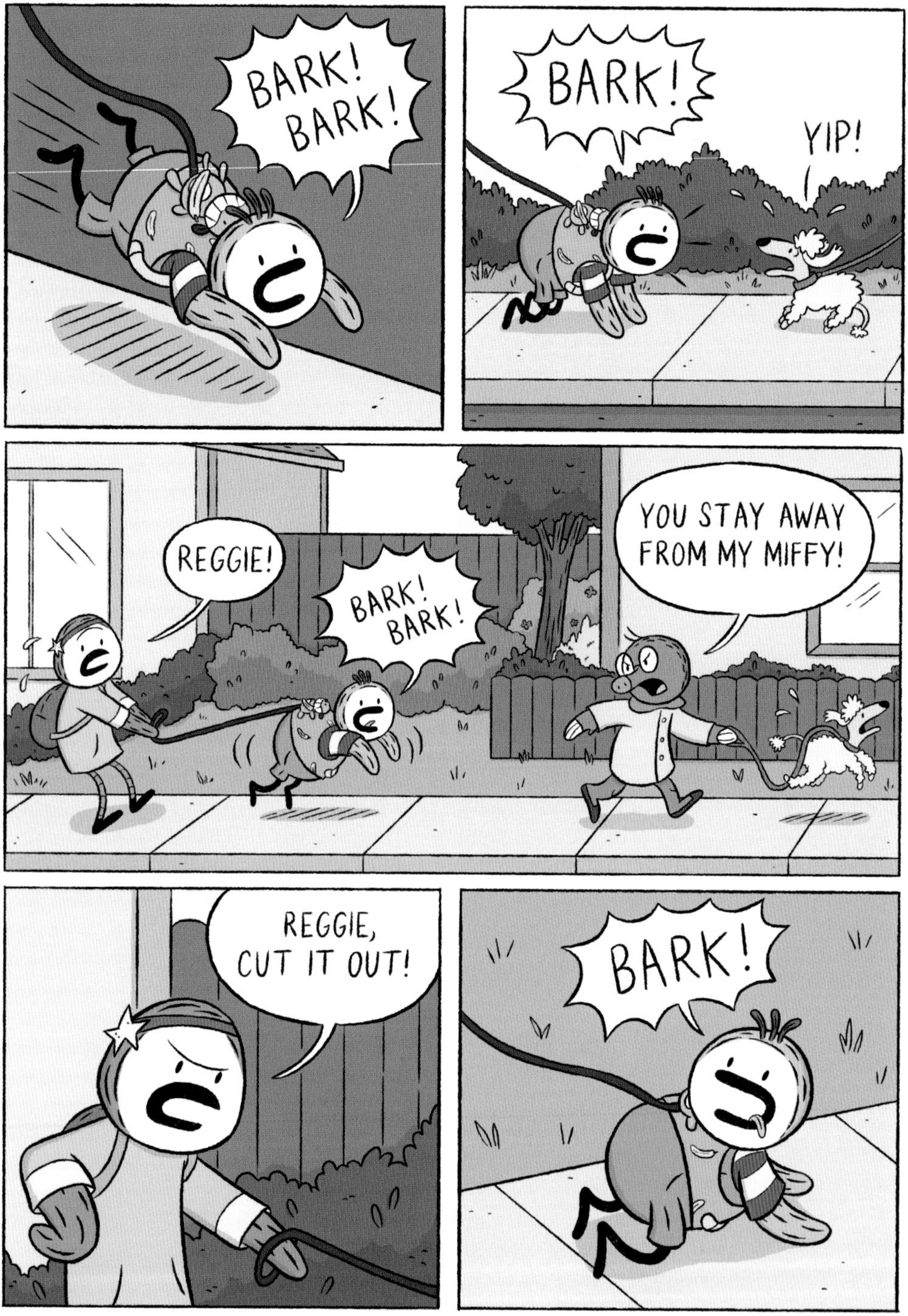
BARK!
BARK!
BARK!
YIP!
REGGIE!
BARK!
BARK!
YOU STAY AWAY
FROM MY MIFFY!
REGGIE,
CUT IT OUT!
BARK!

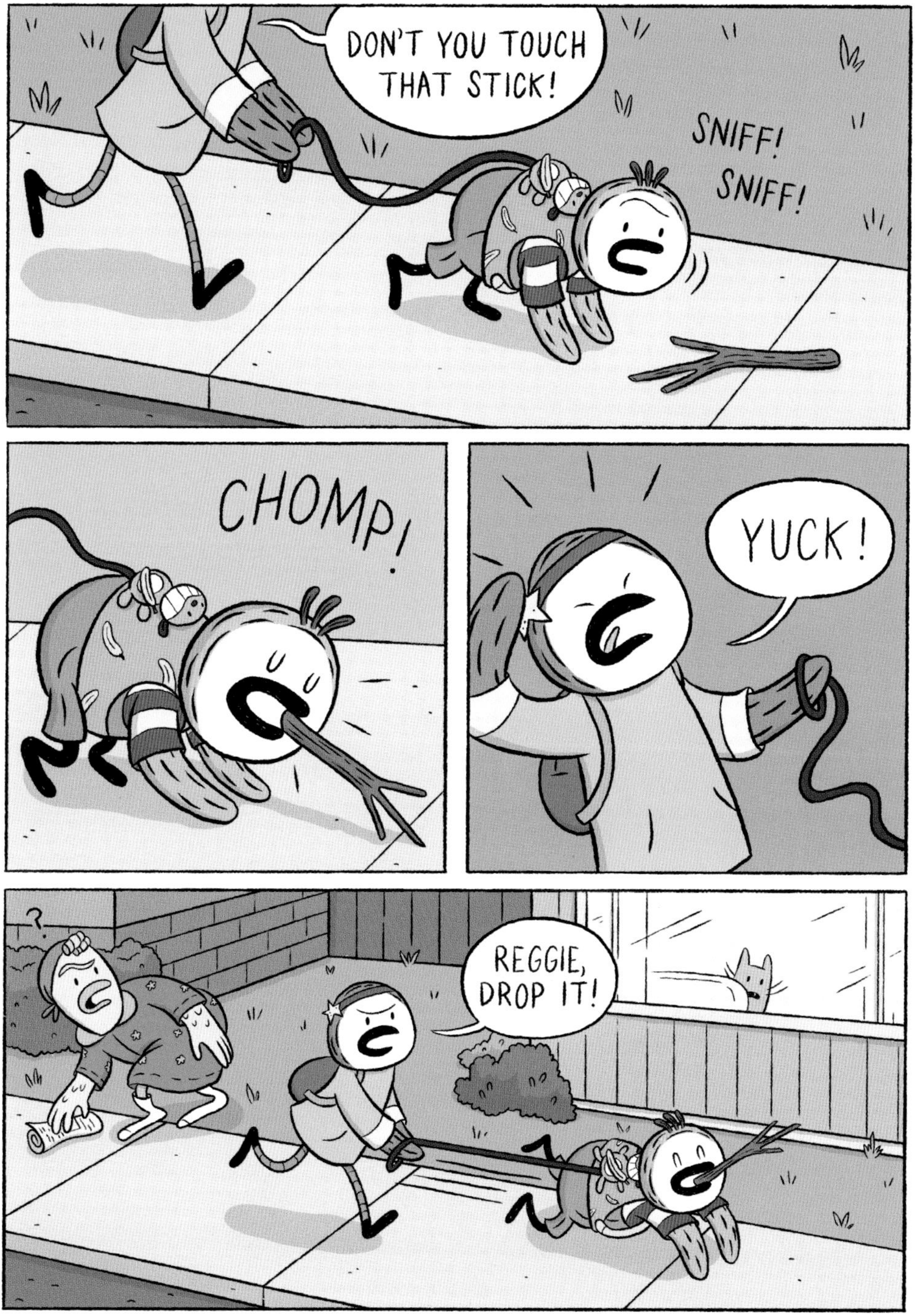

DON'T YOU TOUCH THAT STICK!
SNIFF! SNIFF!
CHOMP!
YUCK!
?
REGGIE, DROP IT!

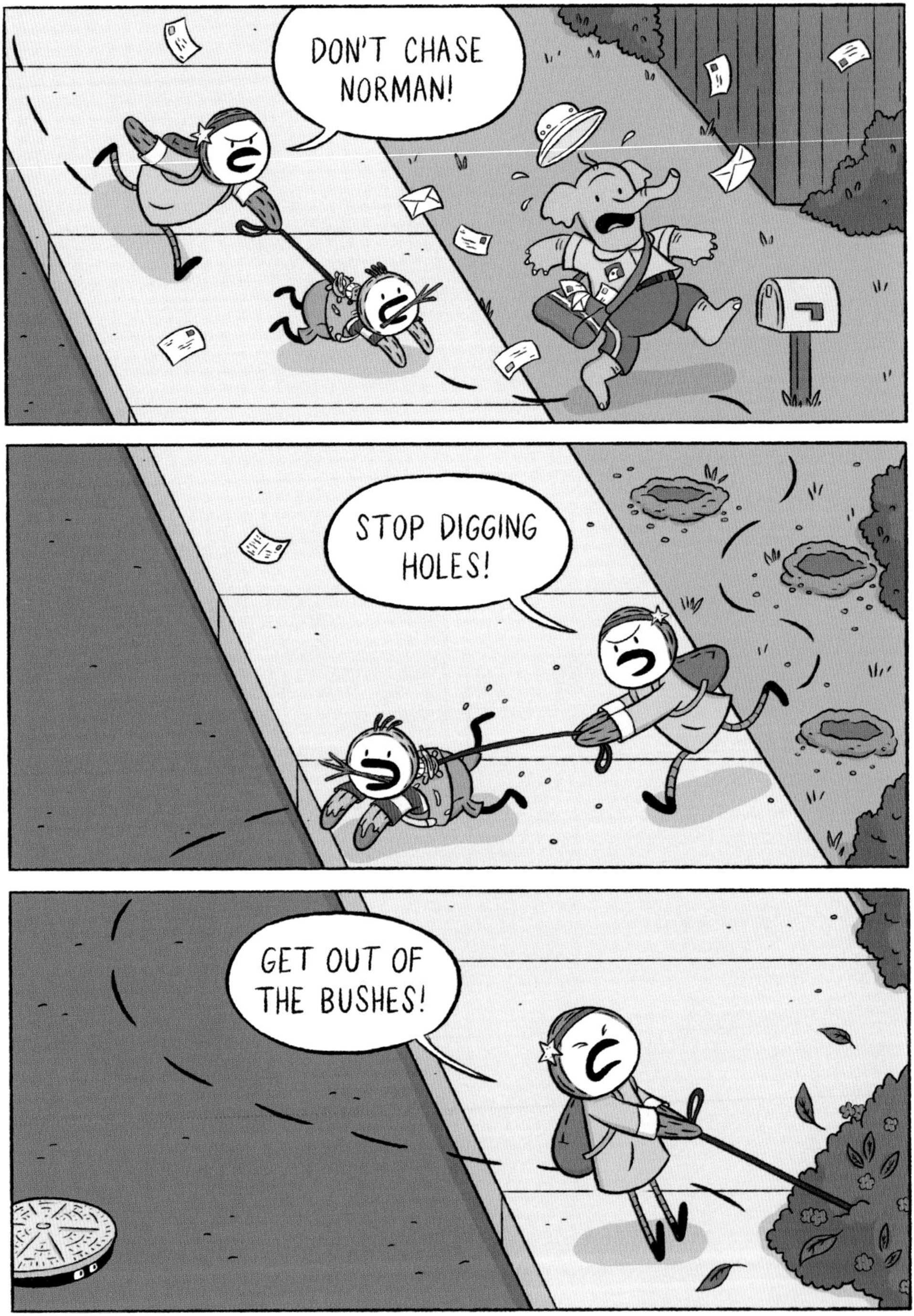
DON'T CHASE NORMAN!
STOP DIGGING HOLES!
GET OUT OF THE BUSHES!

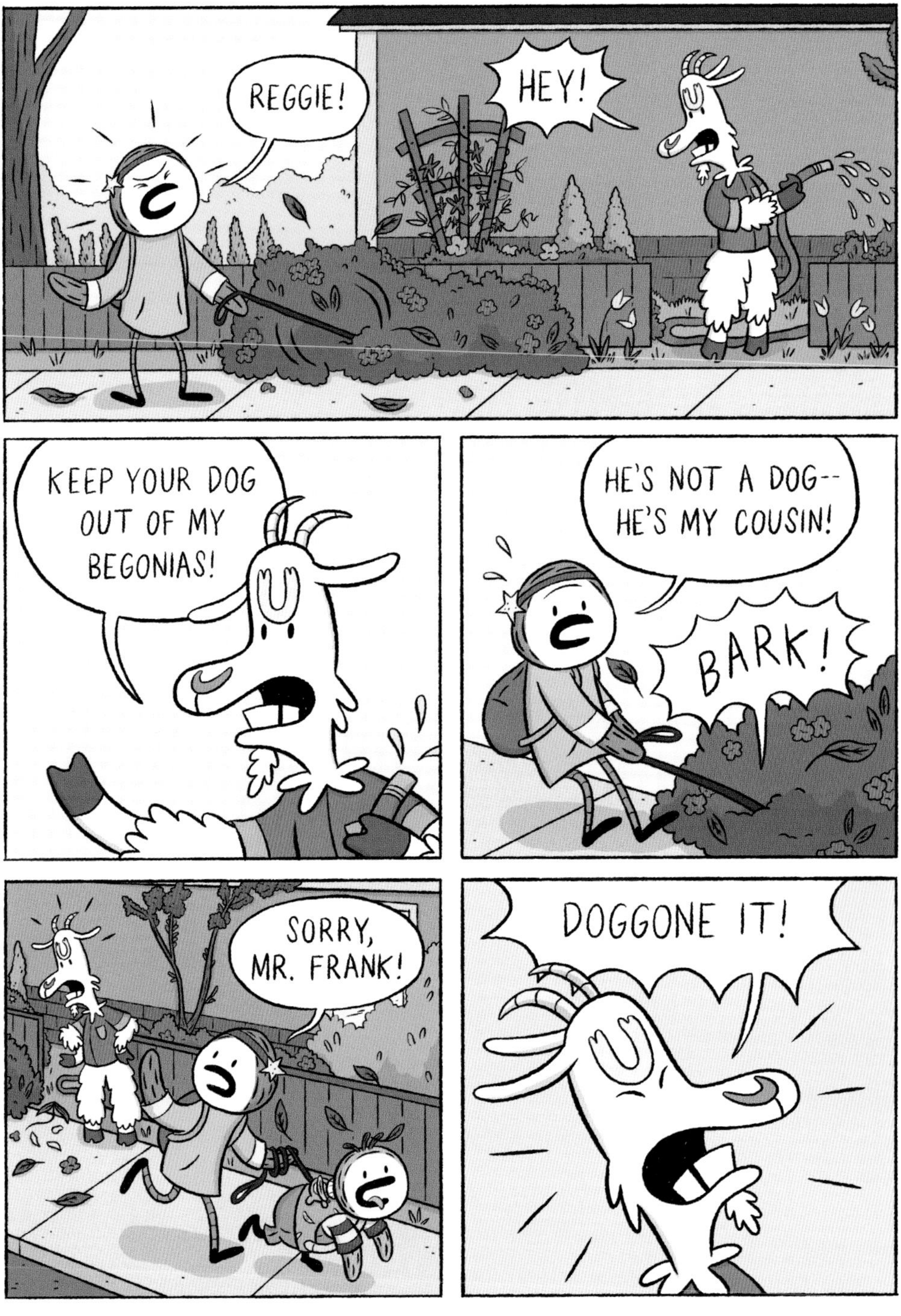
REGGIE!
HEY!
KEEP YOUR DOG OUT OF MY BEGONIAS!
HE'S NOT A DOG-- HE'S MY COUSIN!
BARK!
SORRY, MR. FRANK!
DOGGONE IT!

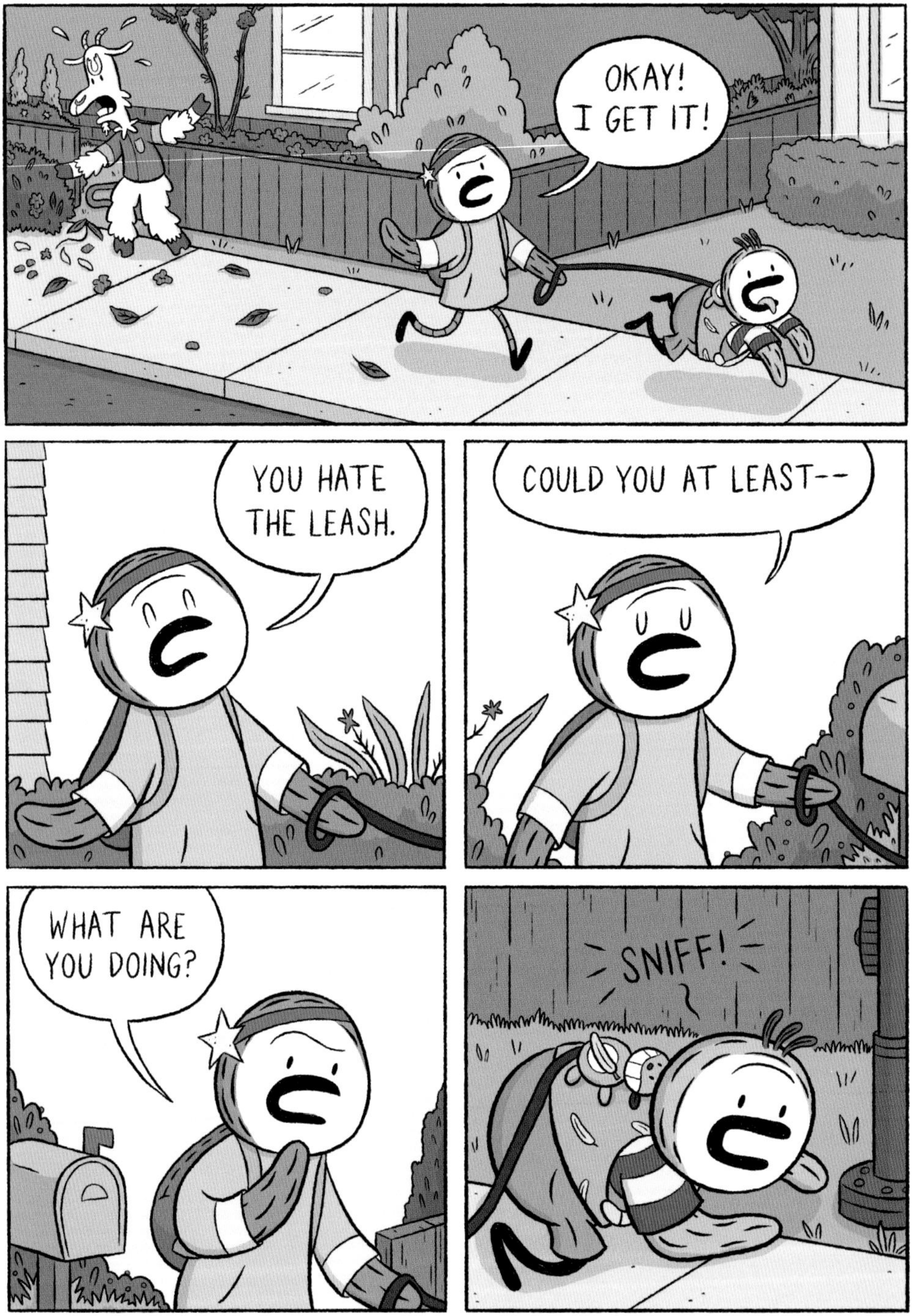
OKAY! I GET IT!
YOU HATE THE LEASH.
COULD YOU AT LEAST--
WHAT ARE YOU DOING?
SNIFF!

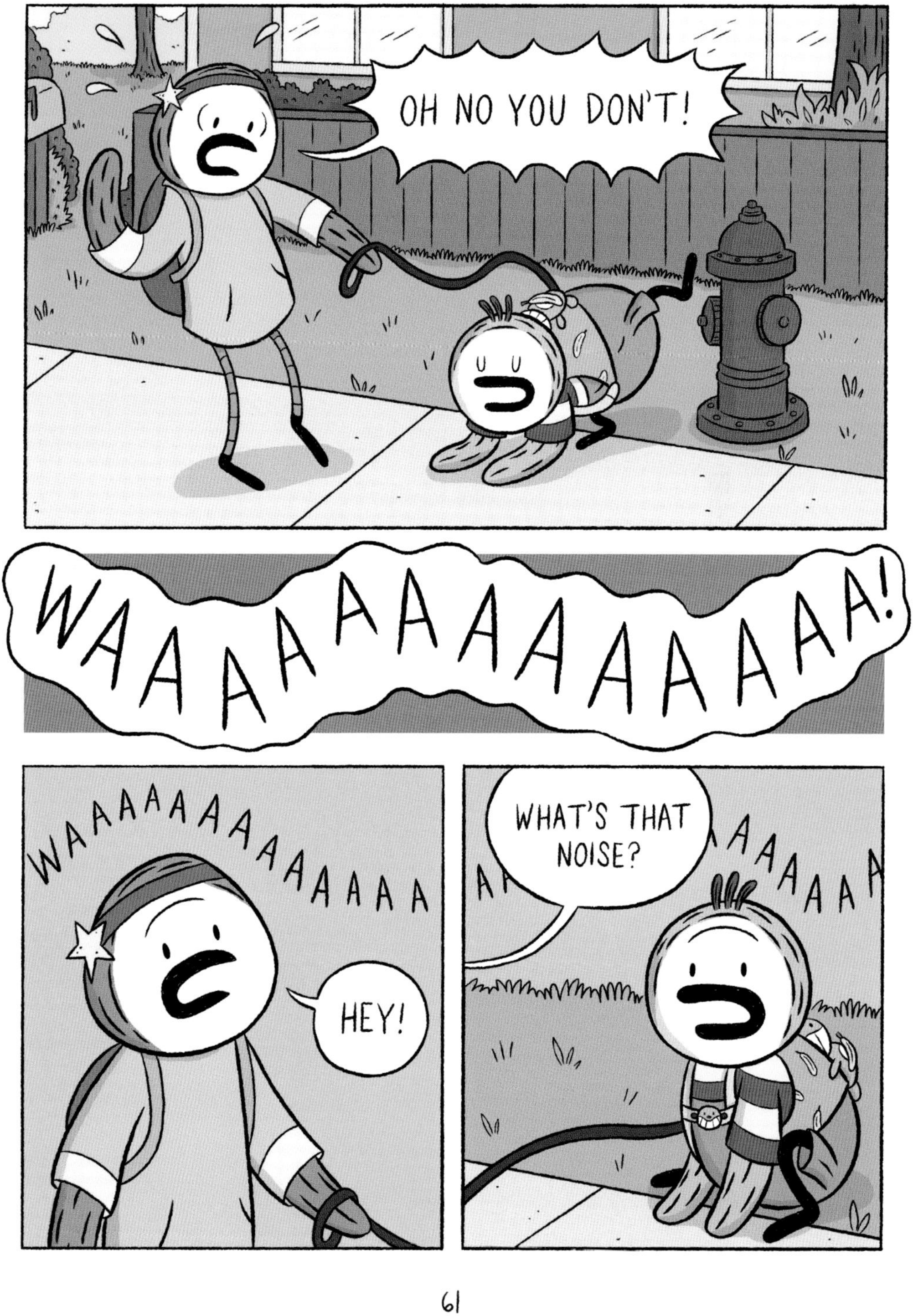
OH NO YOU DON'T!
WAAAAAAAAAAAAA!
WAAAAAAAAAAAAA
HEY!
WHAT'S THAT NOISE?

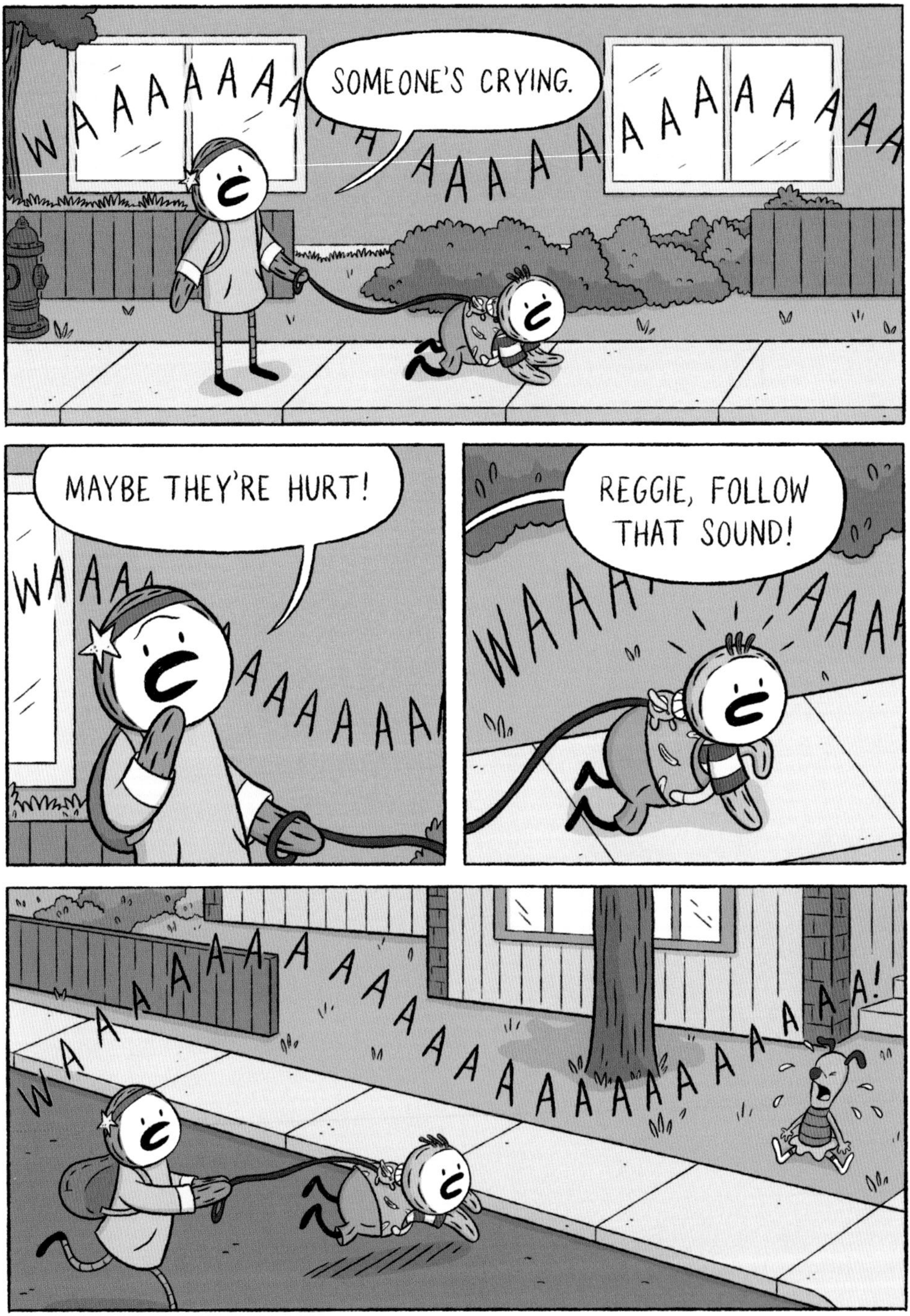
SOMEONE'S CRYING.
MAYBE THEY'RE HURT!
REGGIE, FOLLOW THAT SOUND!

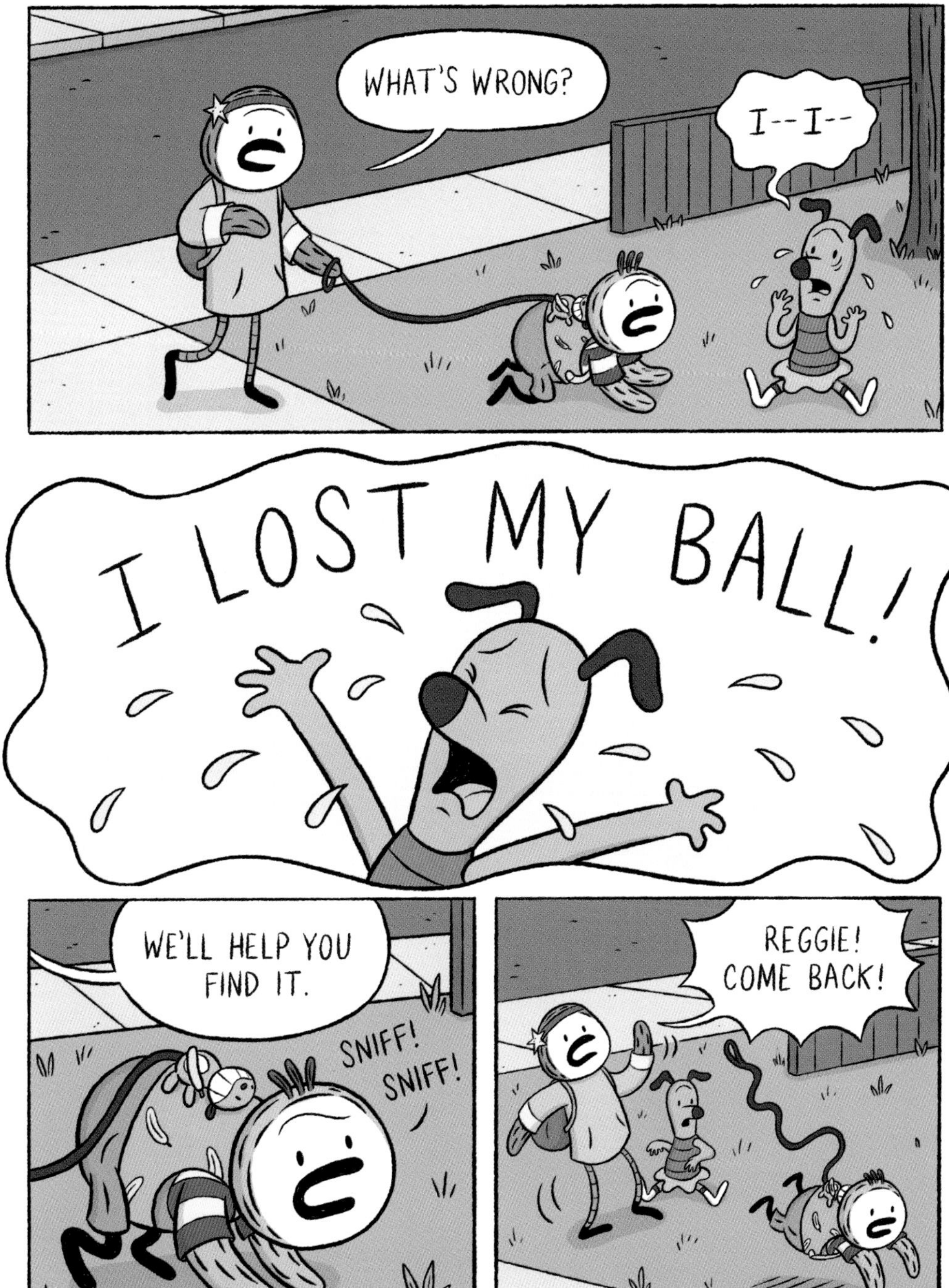
WHAT'S WRONG?
I-- I--
I LOST MY BALL!
WE'LL HELP YOU FIND IT.
SNIFF! SNIFF!
REGGIE! COME BACK!

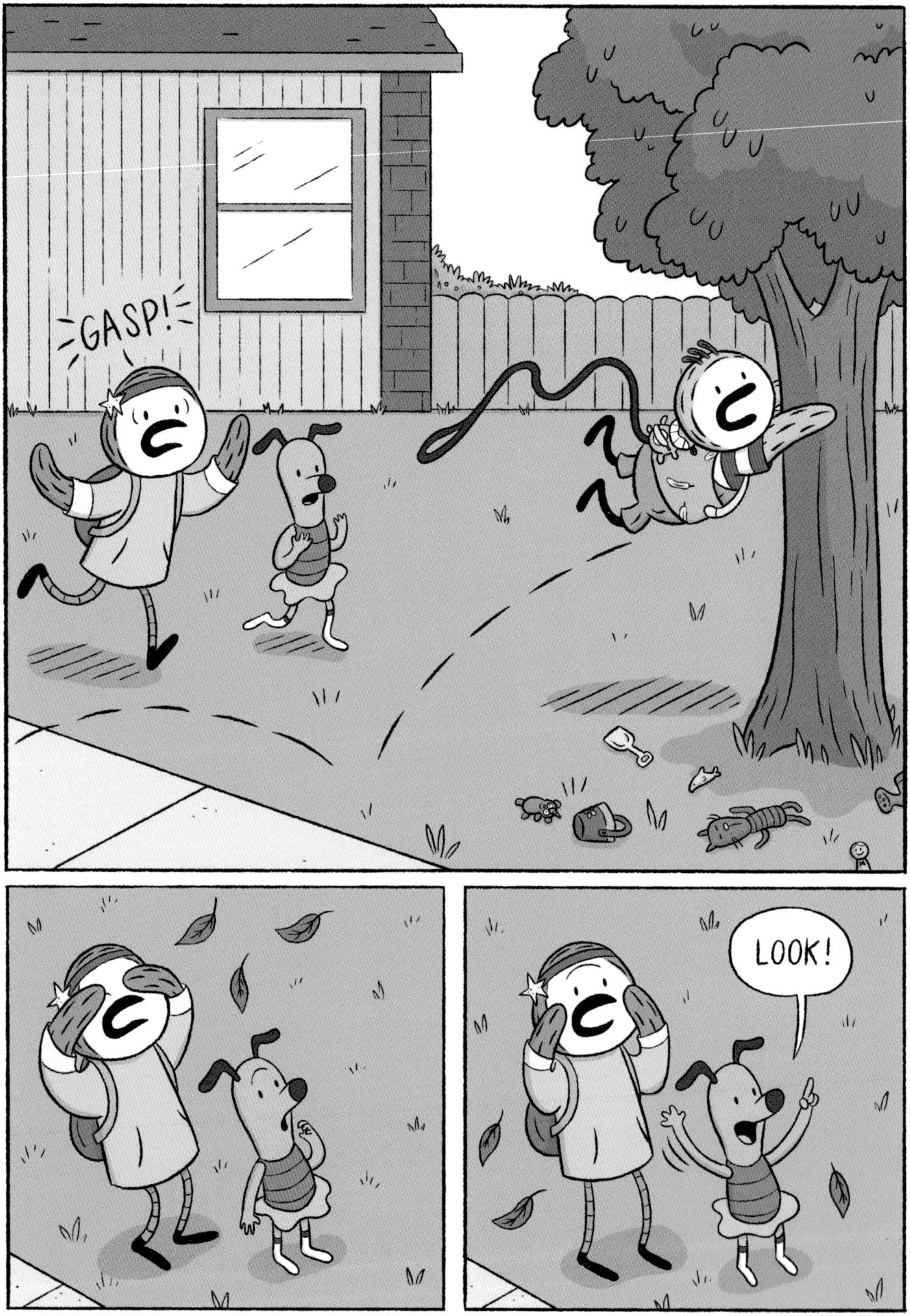
GASP!
LOOK!

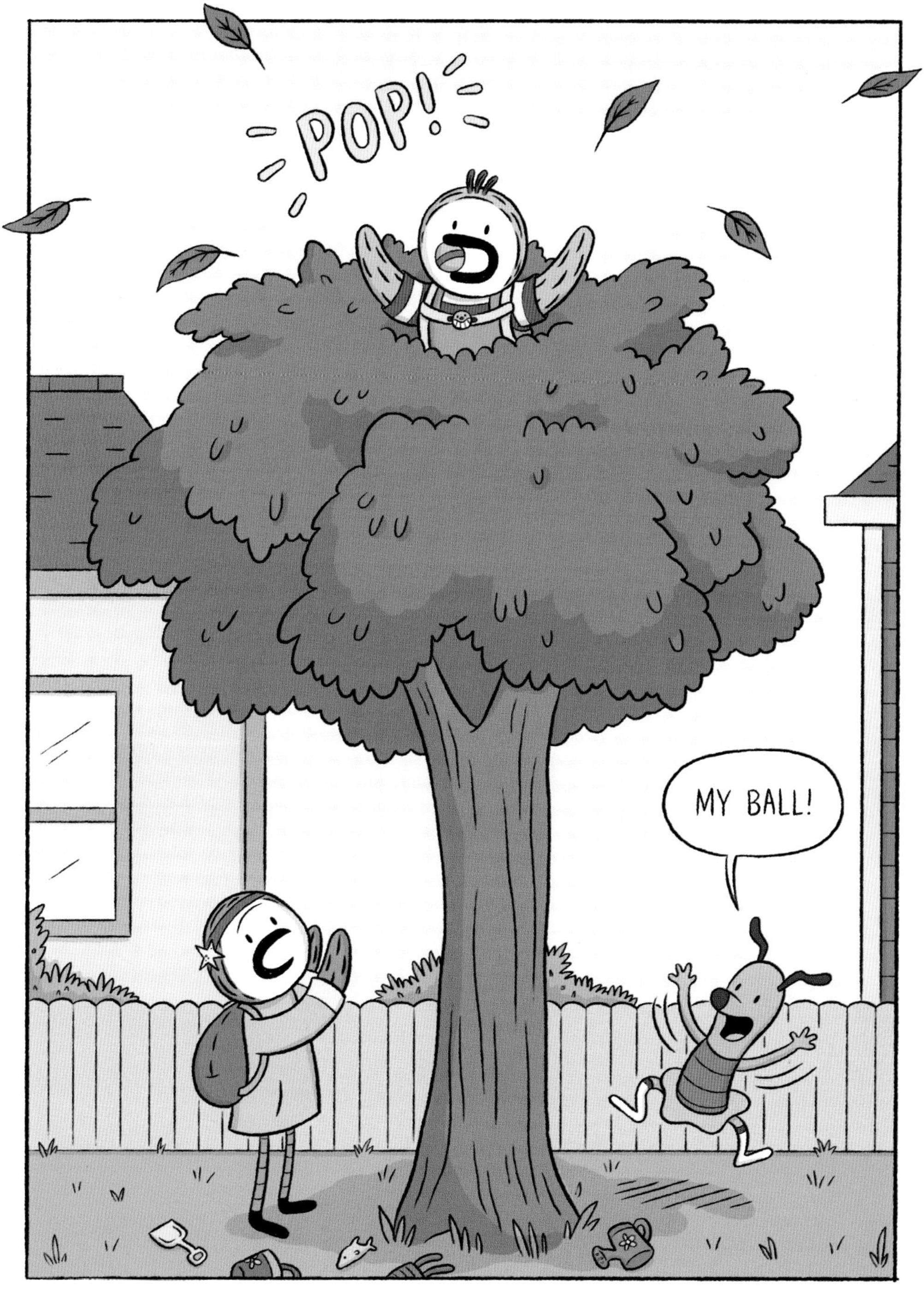
POP!
MY BALL!

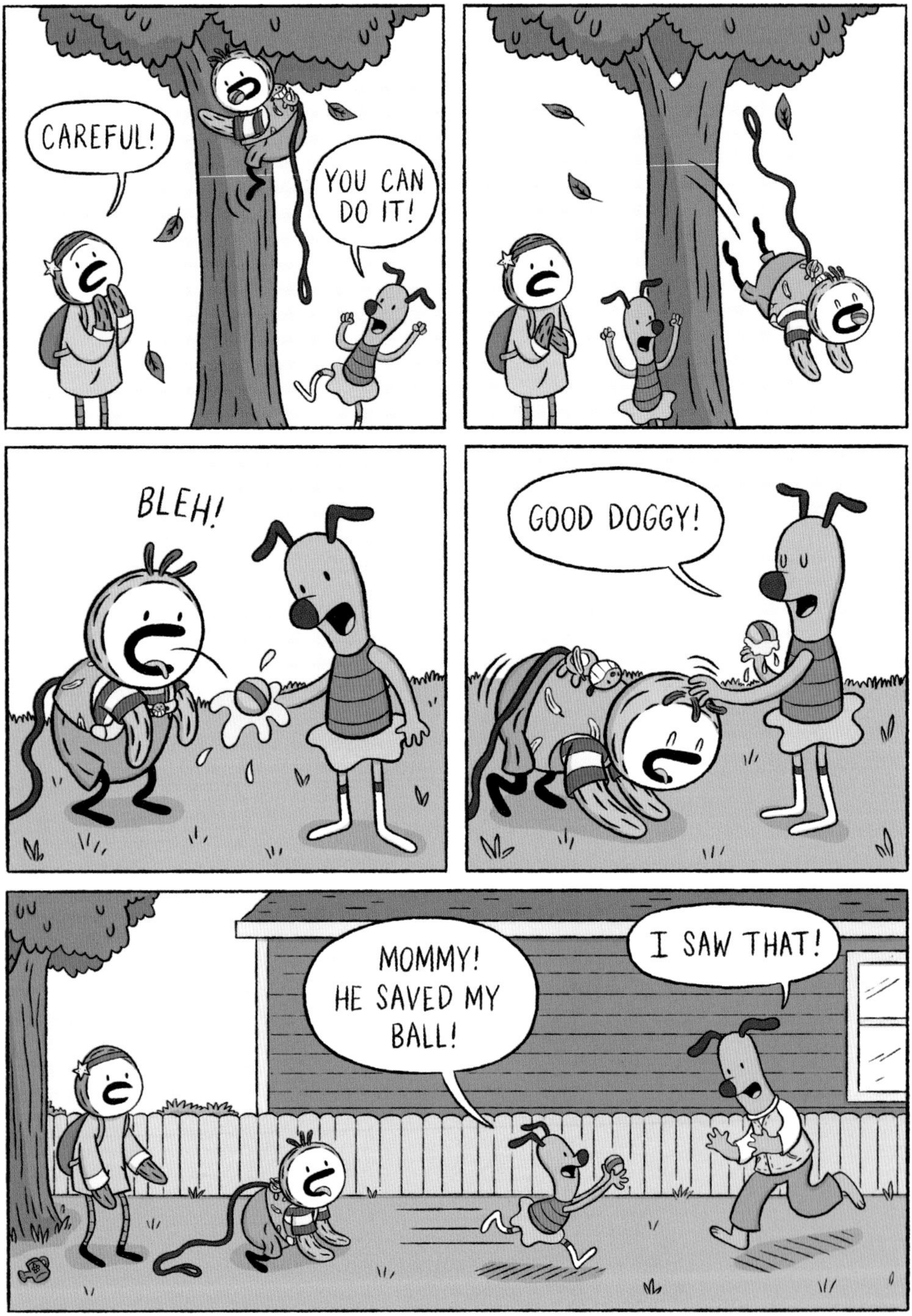
CAREFUL!
YOU CAN DO IT!
BLEH!
GOOD DOGGY!
MOMMY! HE SAVED MY BALL!
I SAW THAT!

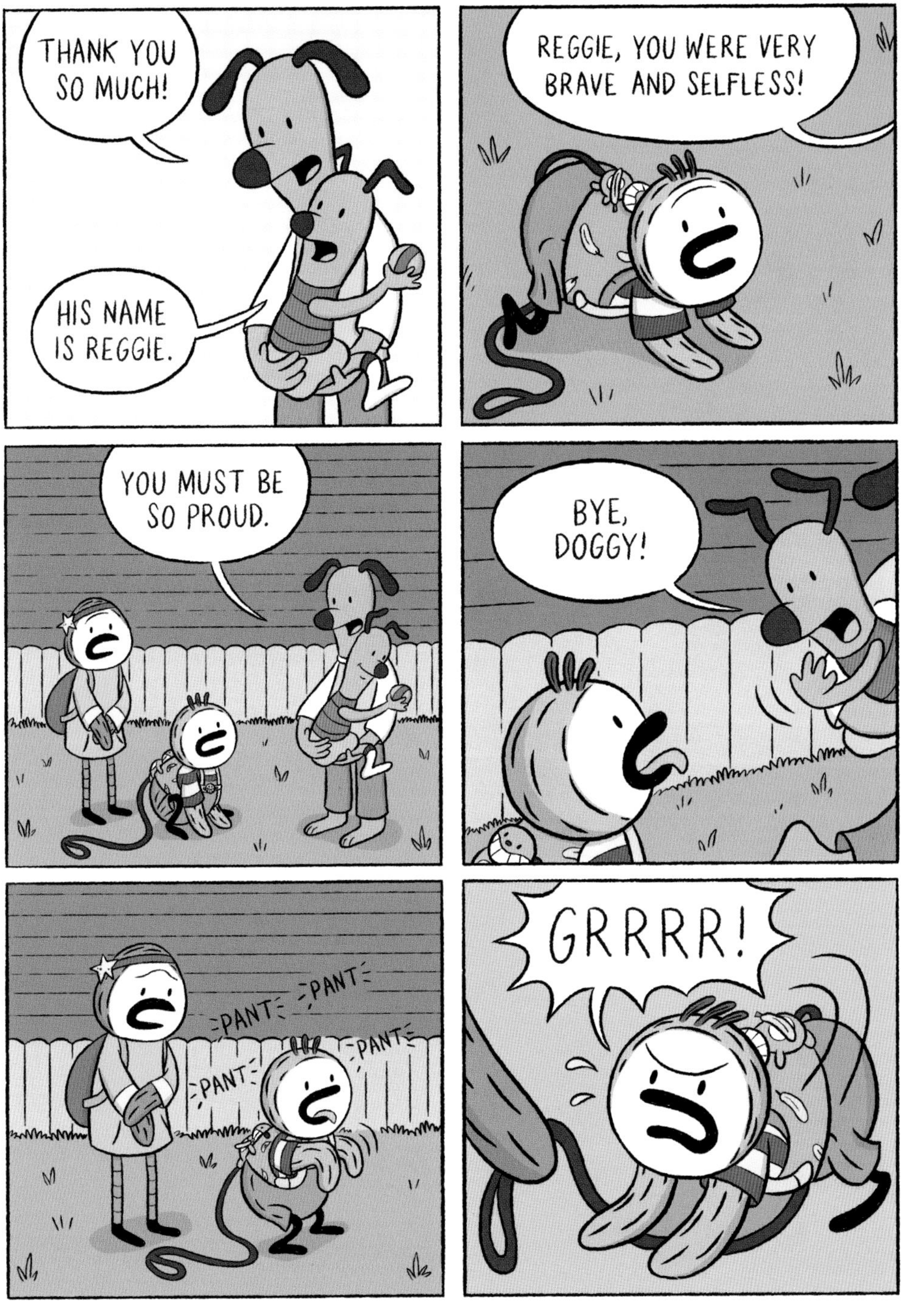
THANK YOU SO MUCH!
HIS NAME IS REGGIE.
REGGIE, YOU WERE VERY BRAVE AND SELFLESS!
YOU MUST BE SO PROUD.
BYE, DOGGY!
PANT
PANT
PANT
PANT
GRRRR!

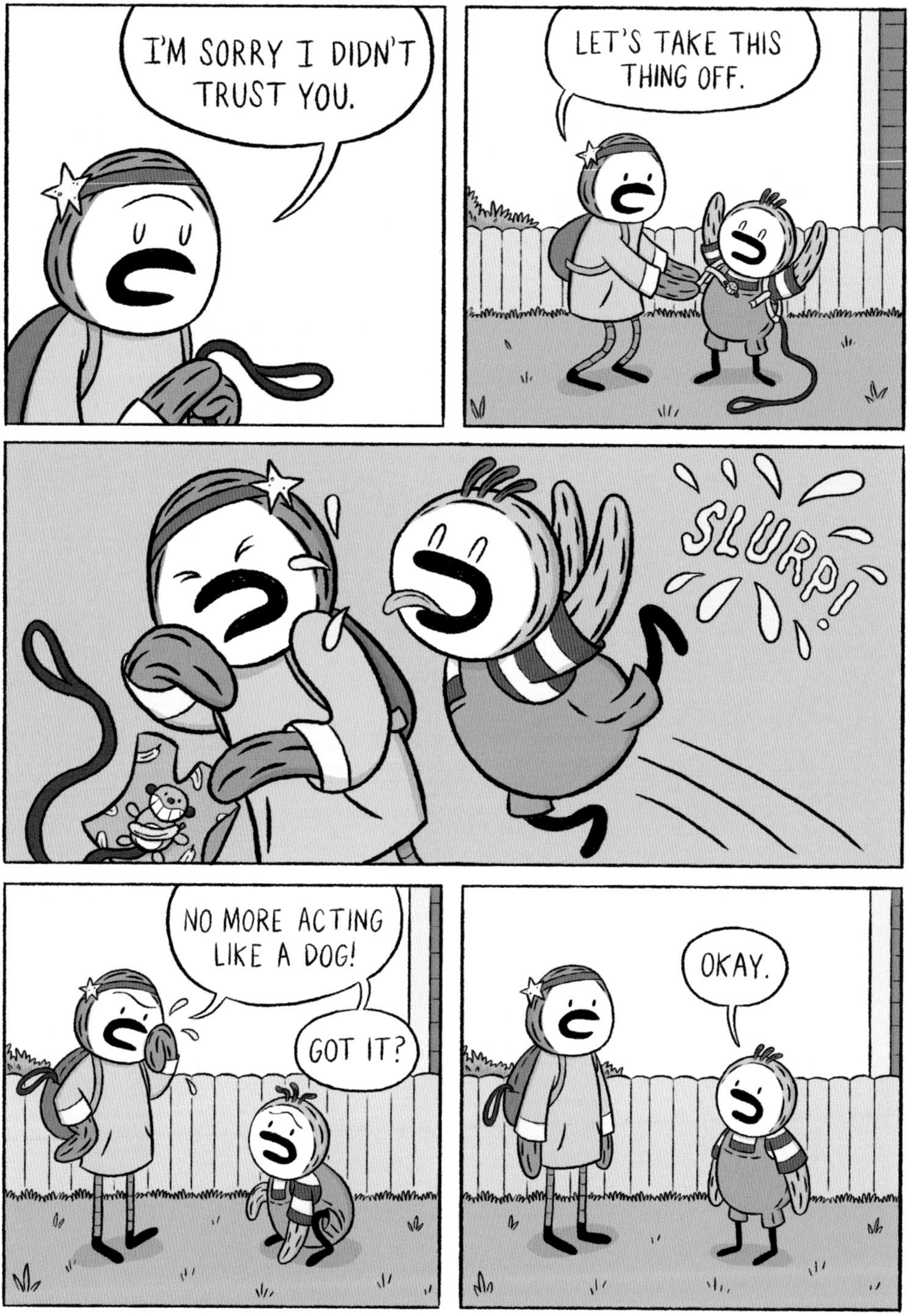
I'M SORRY I DIDN'T TRUST YOU.
LET'S TAKE THIS THING OFF.
SLURP!
NO MORE ACTING LIKE A DOG!
GOT IT?
OKAY.

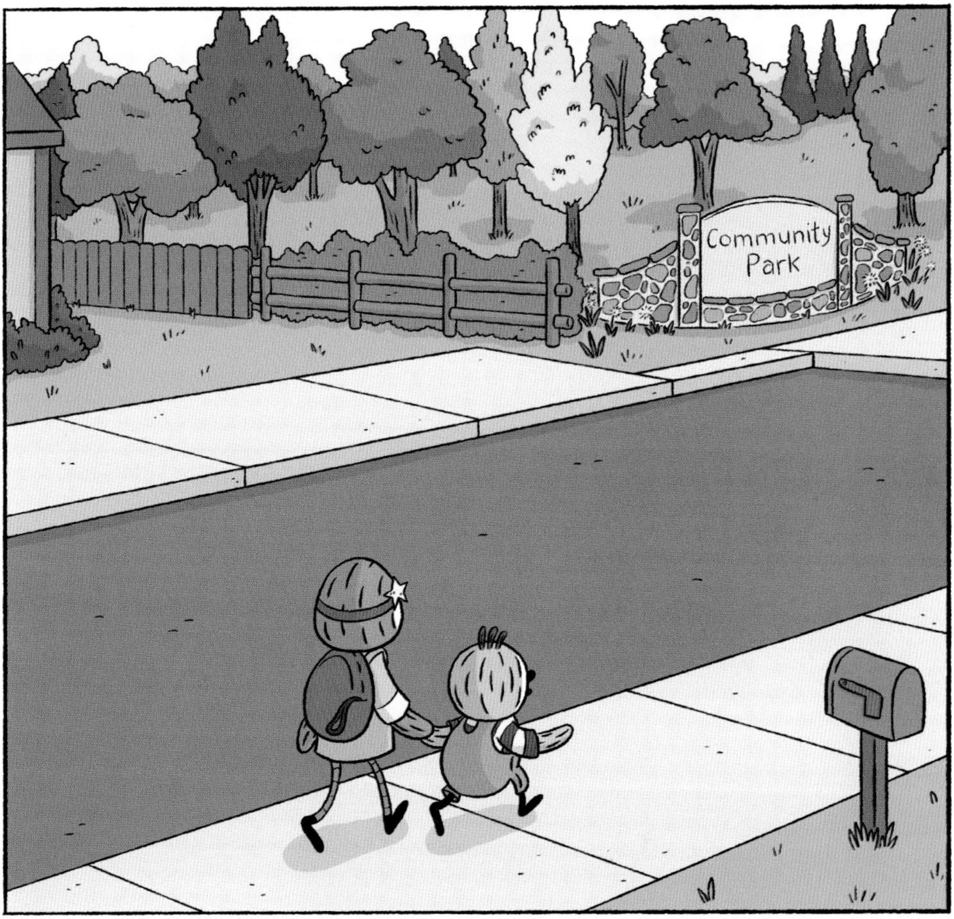
Community
Park

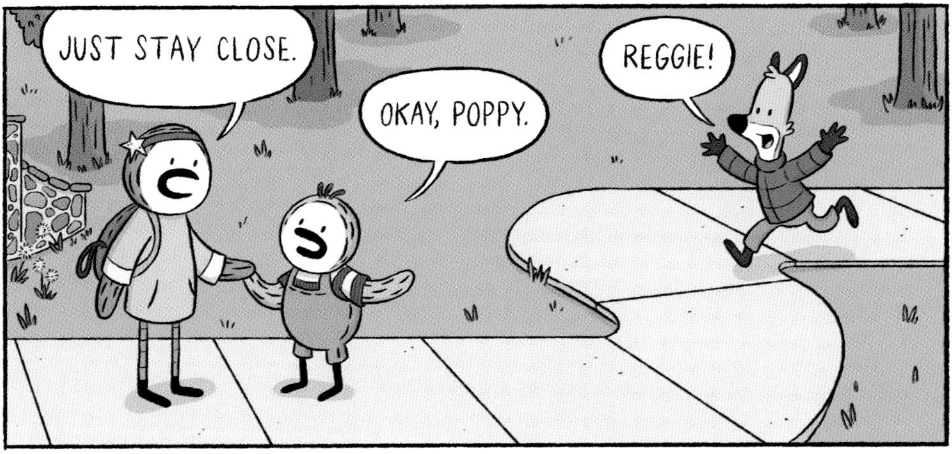
JUST STAY CLOSE.
OKAY, POPPY.
REGGIE!

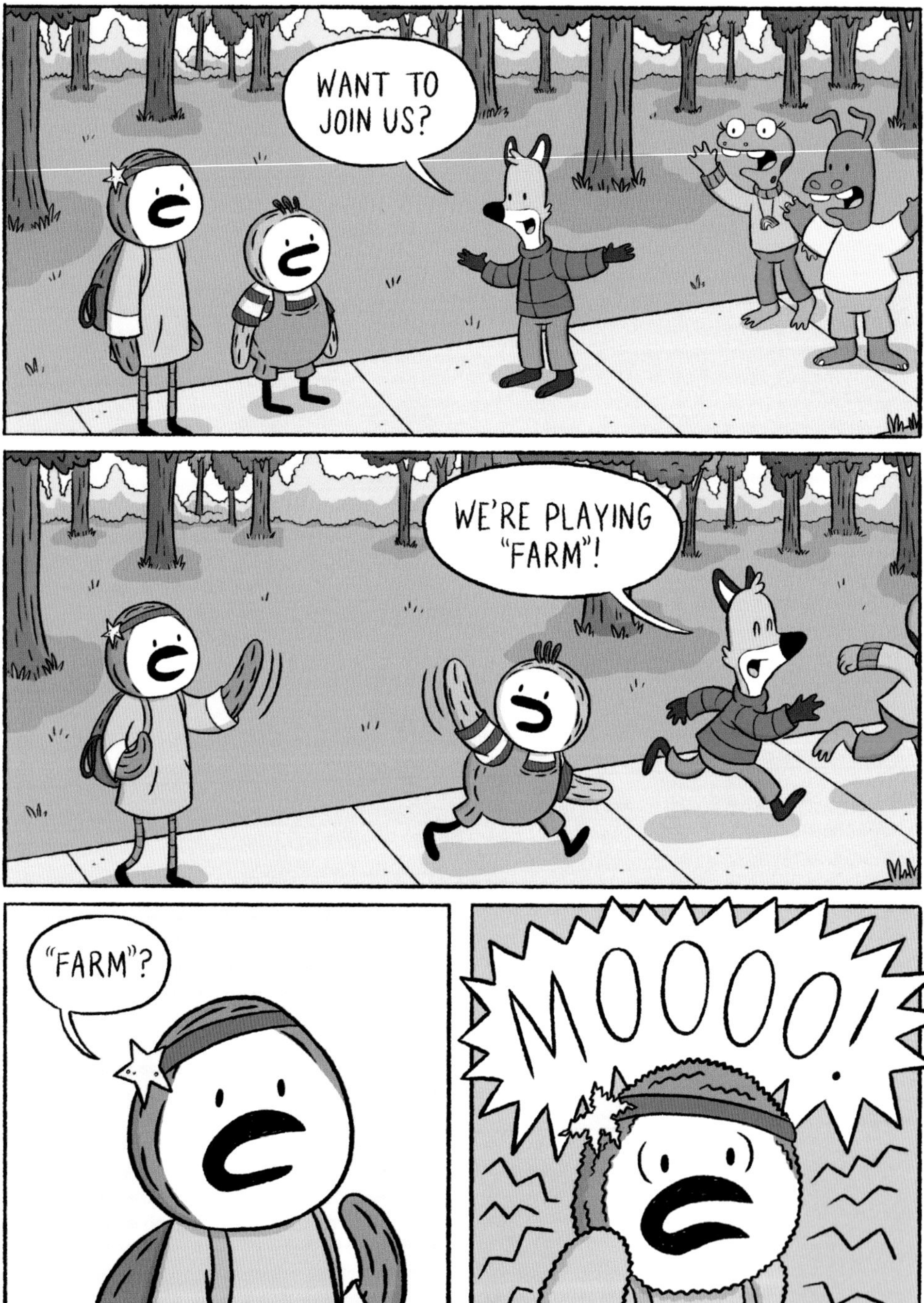
WANT TO JOIN US?
WE'RE PLAYING "FARM"!
"FARM"?
MOOOOO!

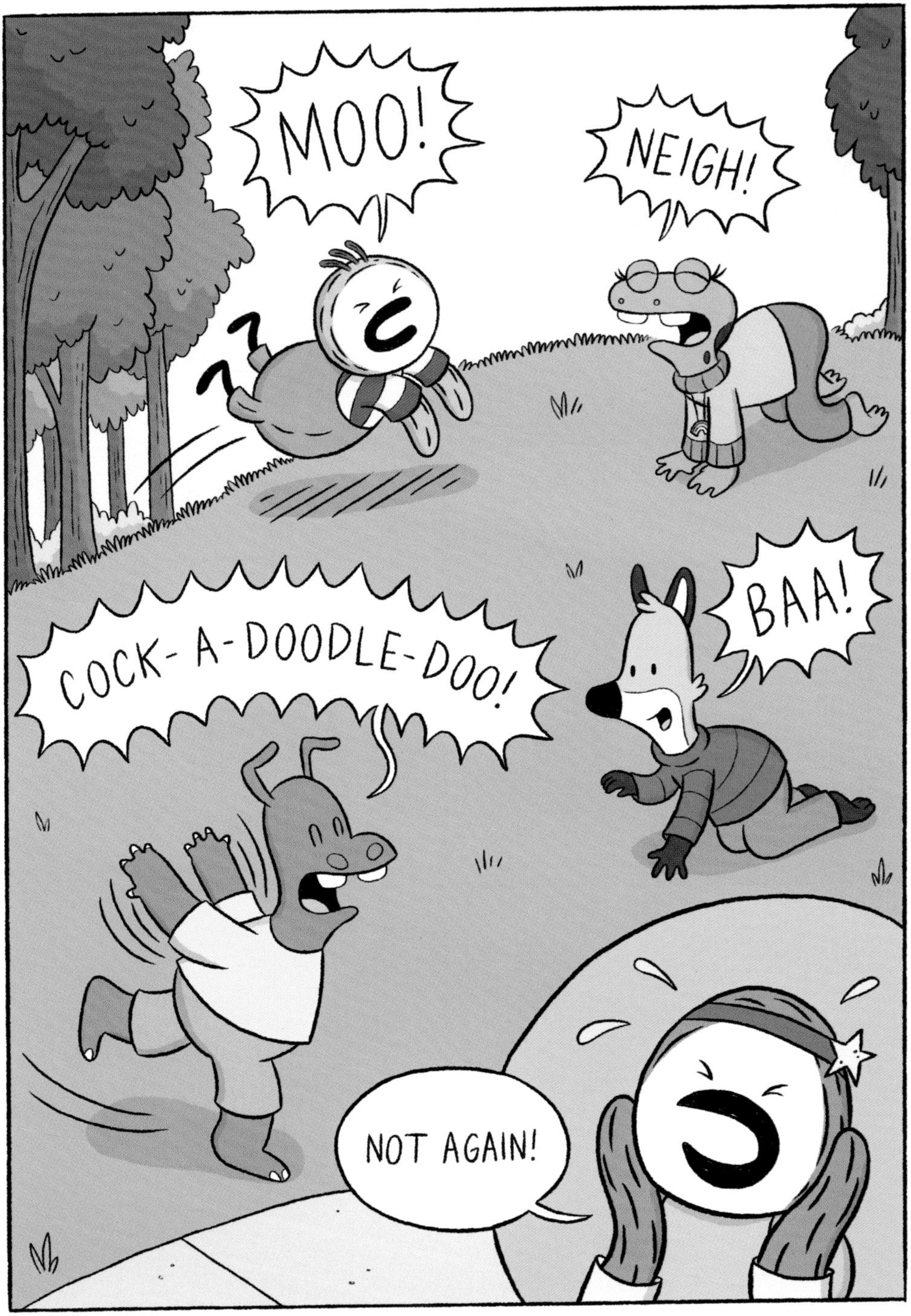
MOO!
NEIGH!
COCK-A-DOODLE-DOO!
BAA!
NOT AGAIN!

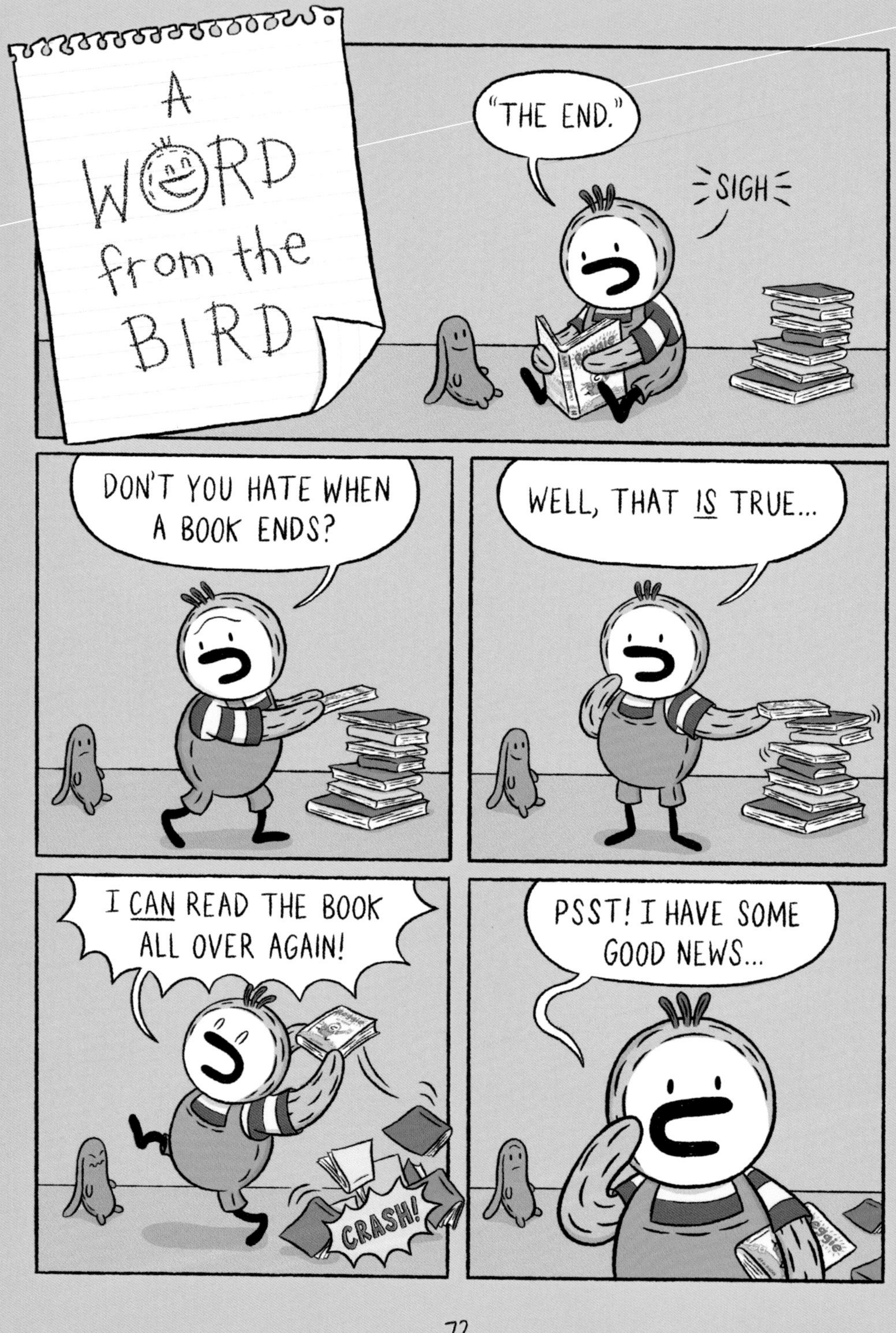
A WORD from the BIRD
"THE END."
SIGH
DON'T YOU HATE WHEN A BOOK ENDS?
WELL, THAT IS TRUE...
I CAN READ THE BOOK ALL OVER AGAIN!
CRASH!
PSST! I HAVE SOME GOOD NEWS...

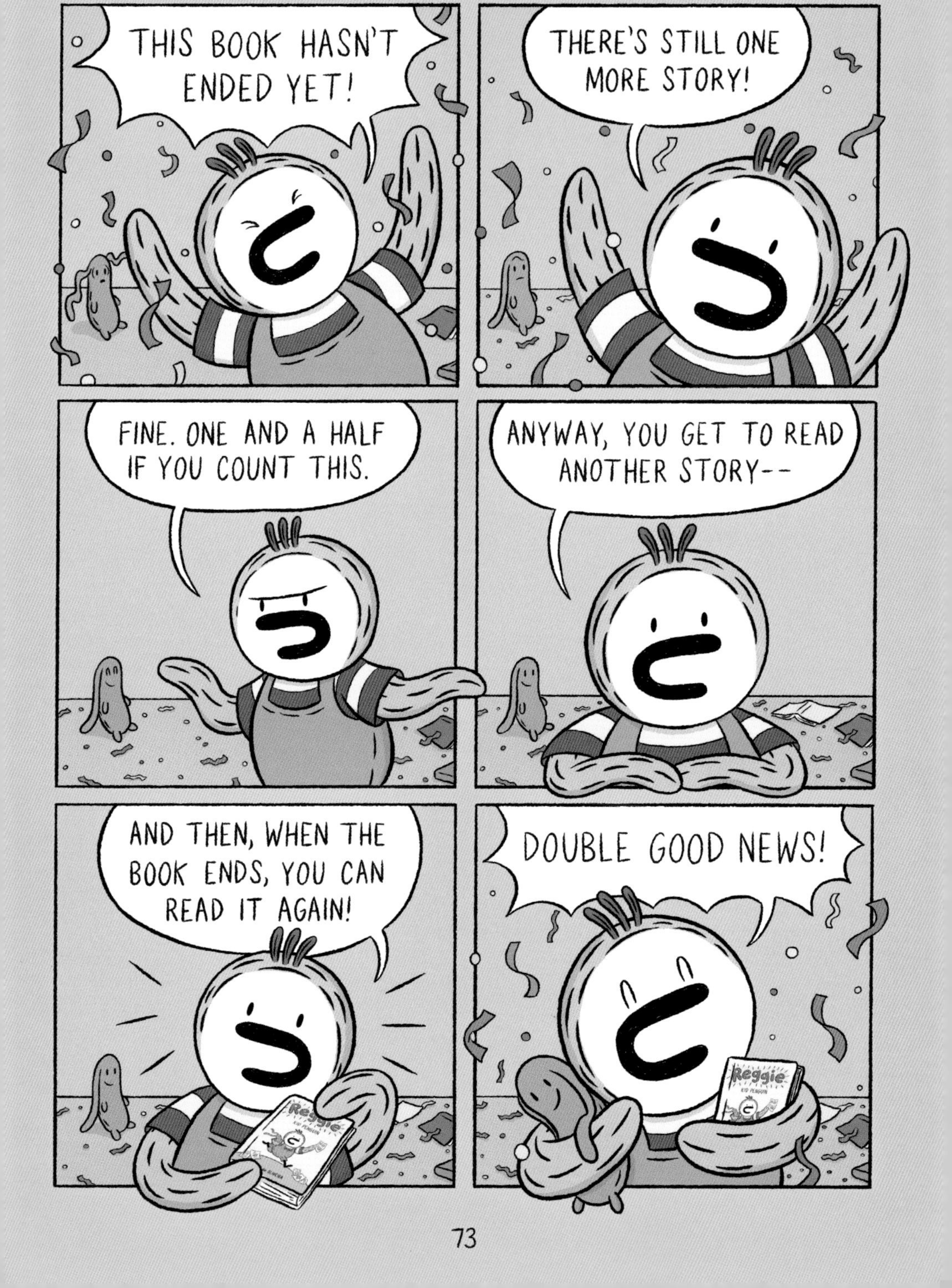
THIS BOOK HASN'T ENDED YET!
THERE'S STILL ONE MORE STORY!
FINE. ONE AND A HALF IF YOU COUNT THIS.
ANYWAY, YOU GET TO READ ANOTHER STORY--
AND THEN, WHEN THE BOOK ENDS, YOU CAN READ IT AGAIN!
DOUBLE GOOD NEWS!

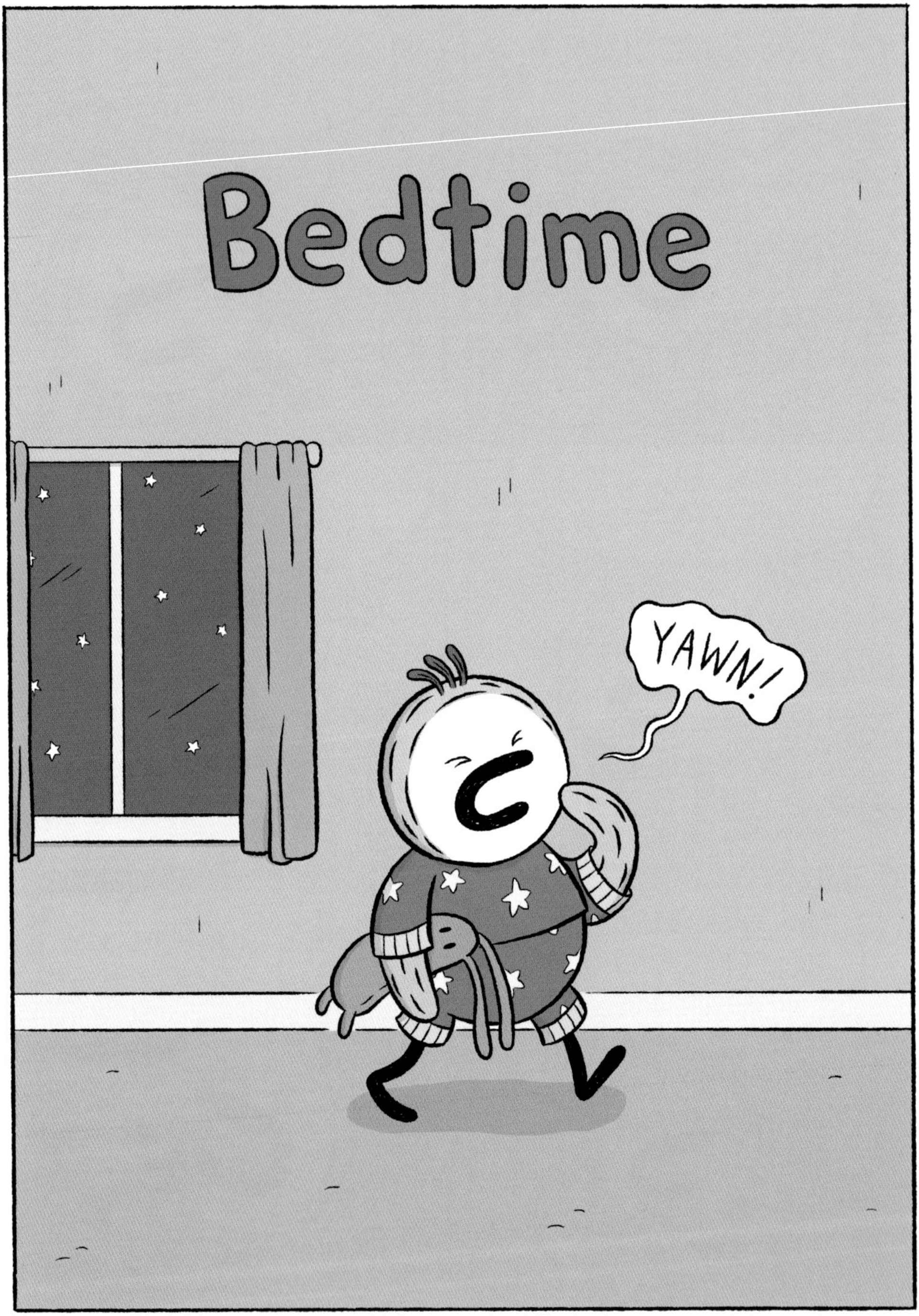
Bedtime
YAWN!

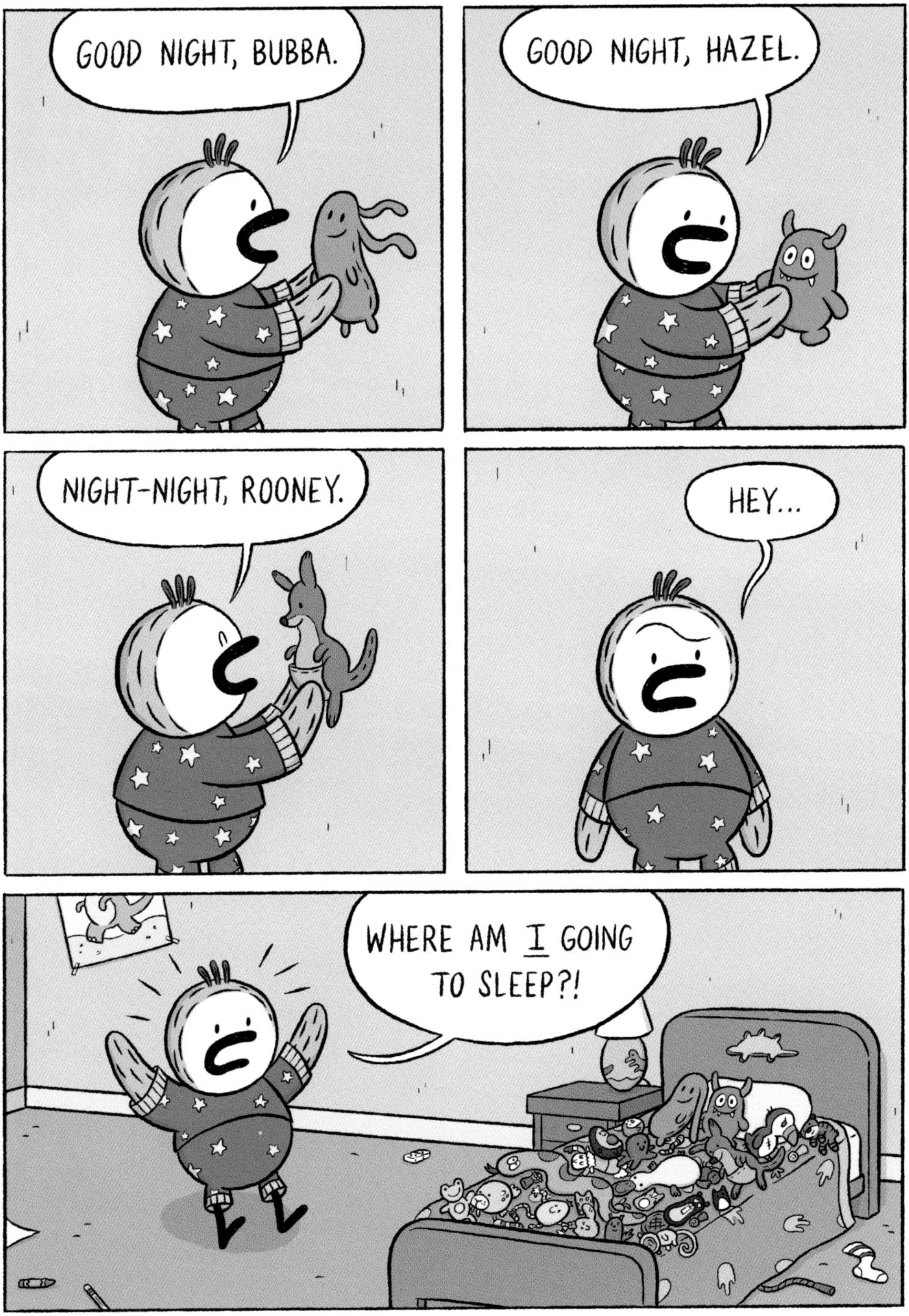
GOOD NIGHT, BUBBA.
GOOD NIGHT, HAZEL.
NIGHT-NIGHT, ROONEY.
HEY...
WHERE AM I GOING TO SLEEP?!

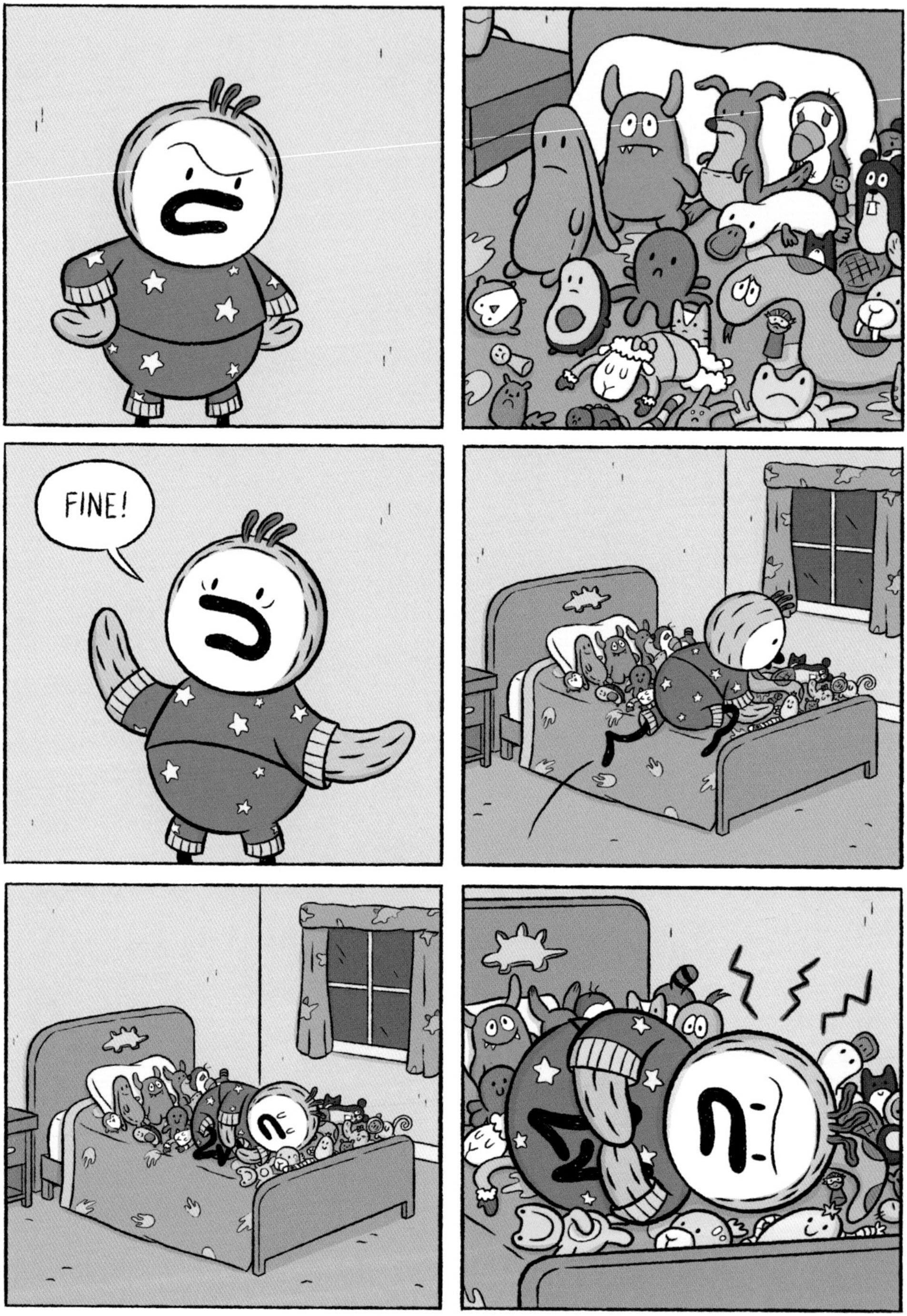
FINE!

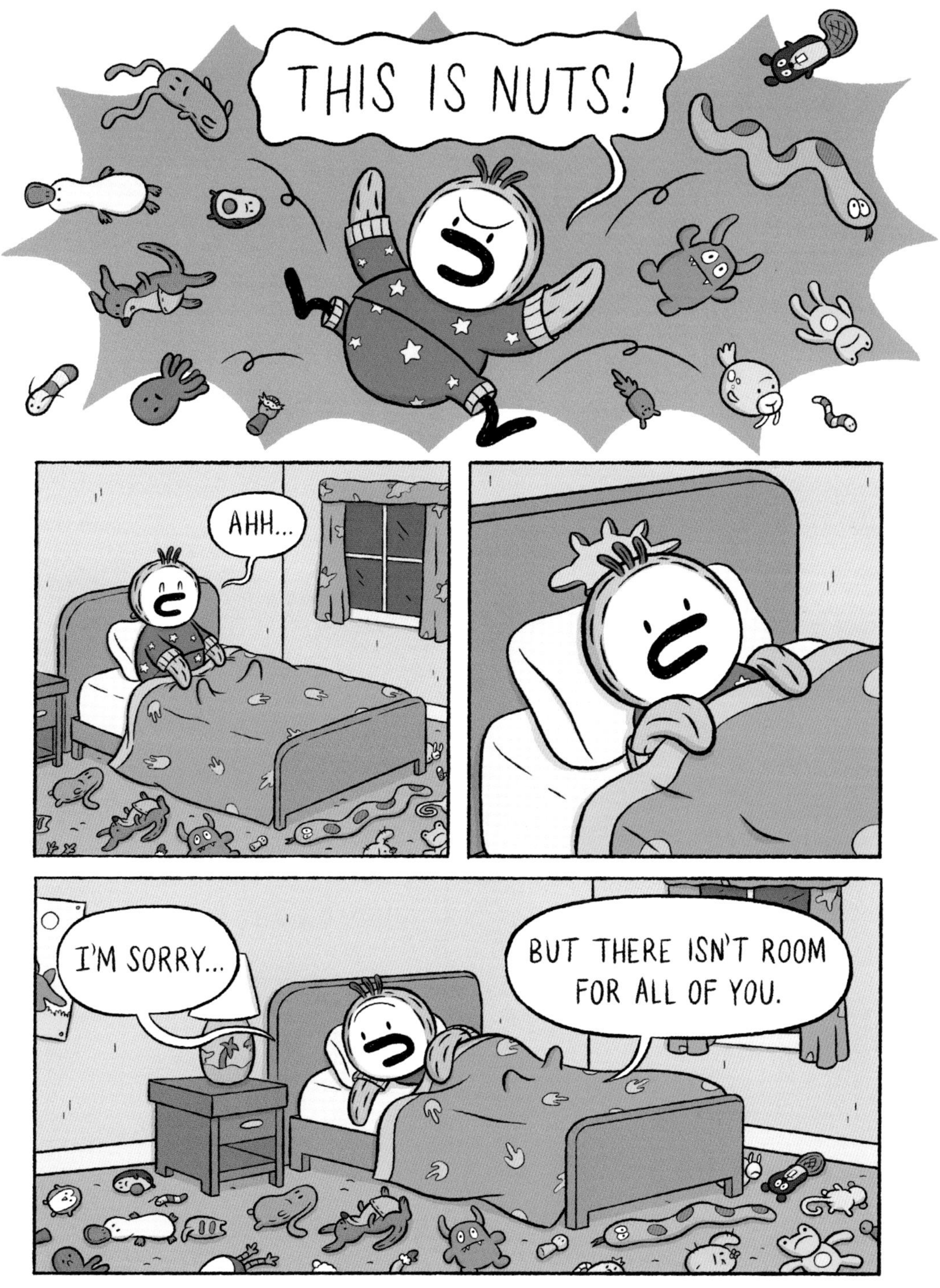
THIS IS NUTS!
AHH...
I'M SORRY...
BUT THERE ISN'T ROOM FOR ALL OF YOU.

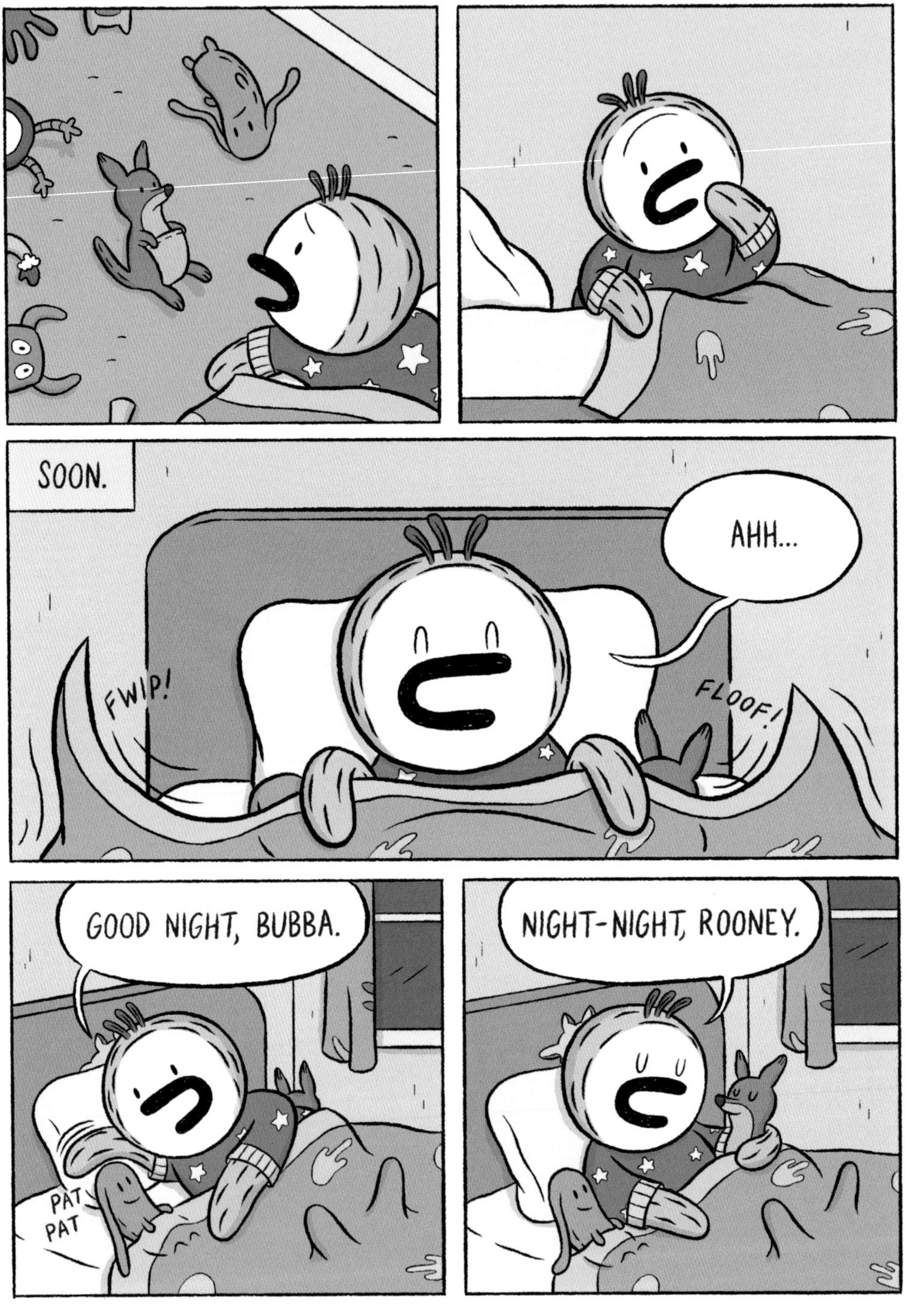
SOON.
AHH...
FWIP!
FLOOF!
GOOD NIGHT, BUBBA.
PAT PAT
NIGHT-NIGHT, ROONEY.

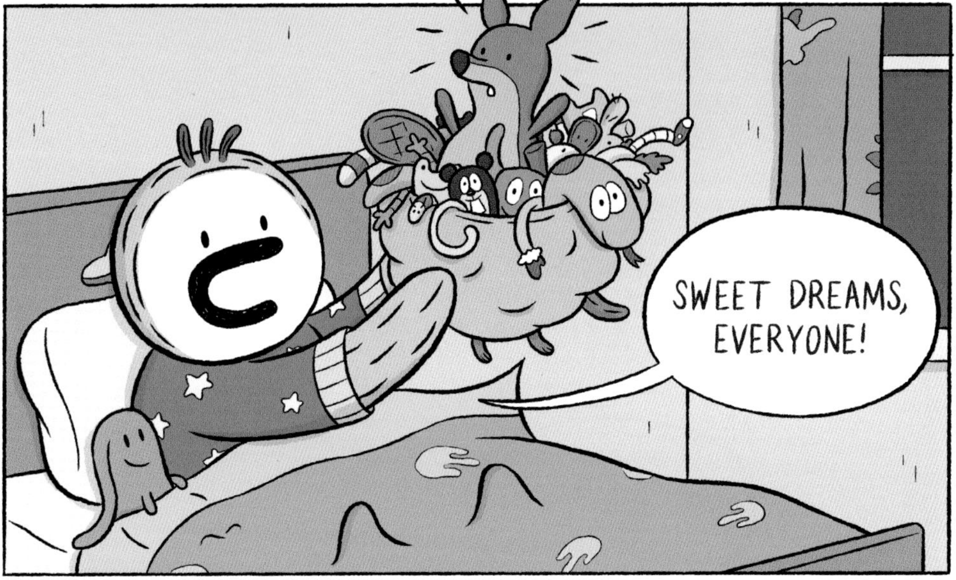
SWEET DREAMS, EVERYONE!

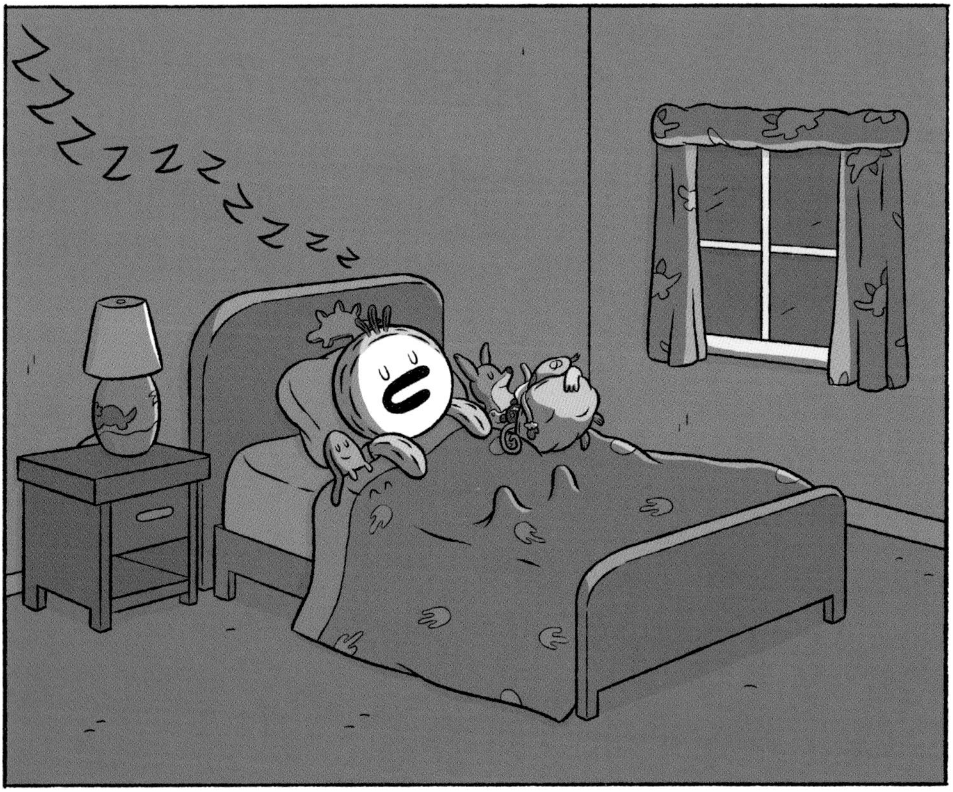
ZZZZZZZZZZZZ

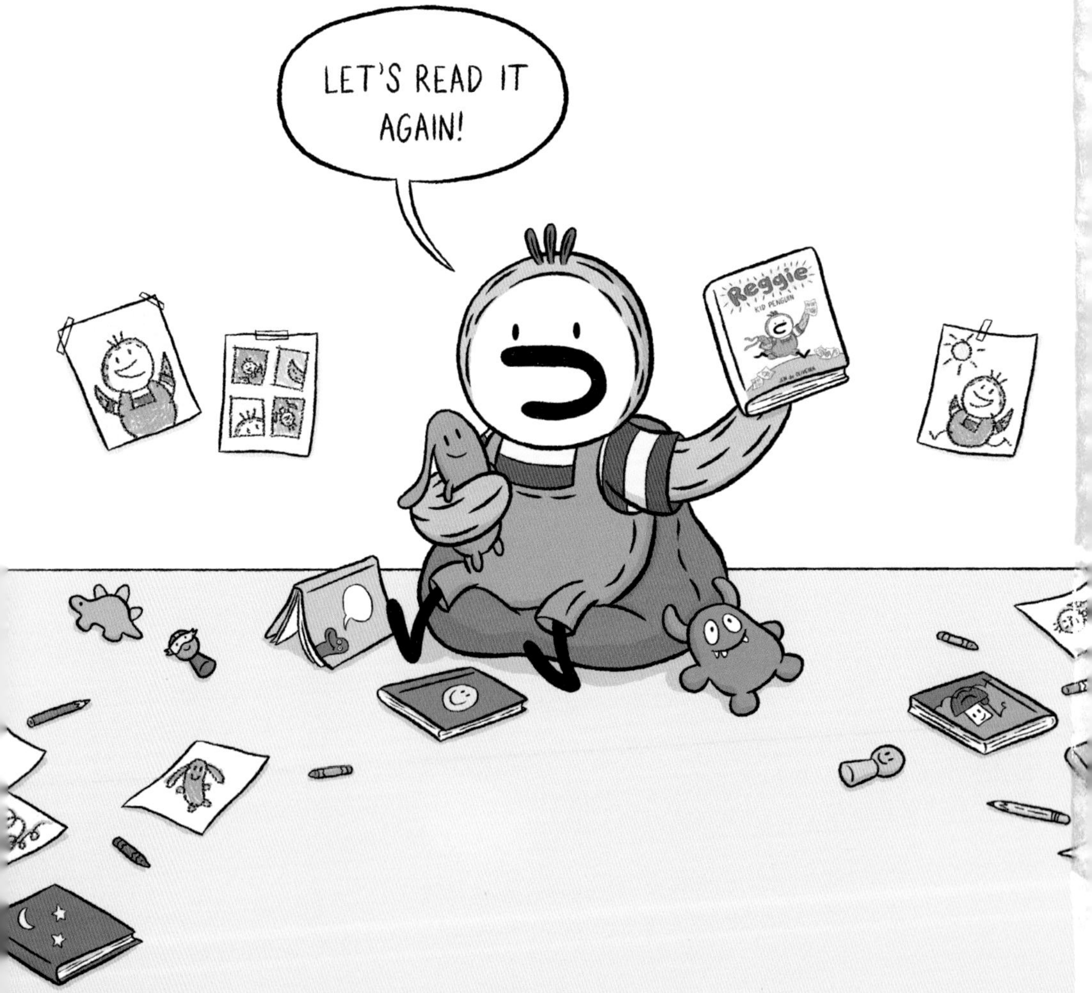
LET'S READ IT AGAIN!
Reggie
KID PENGUIN